Katrina, Rita
&
AN ACADIAN
ODYSSEY

N. J. Jacob, MD

This book obviously is not the DSM. It is a work of fiction.

Disclaimer

All characters in this novel are fictional, any comparison otherwise is just a figment of your imagination.

DEDICATED

To the memory of Mike Schaab

And to all the people, Military and civilian, victim and otherwise, who have suffered the anguish of PTSD.

Acknowledgements

My profound gratitude to the three most important people in my life, my wife Rose, my children Katrina & Ann, who put up with me through the trying times.

My dear friend, Henry Sisk.

Loren H. Roth, MD, without whose help my trip would not have materialized.
Mary Ganguli, MD, my mentor; Eric Rodriguez, MD, my policy advisor. Dr. Paul Kattuman, a la motivator; Sara Miller, MSW, my resident editor.
Dr Rick Morycz, my friend, who gave me courage to take this project forward.
Drs Rob Sweet and Adele Towers, my long term friends.
Michelle Feingold, Rose Marie Pearle, Jennifer Eichhorn and Gerri Hasslett (motivators).
Dr. Umapathy, who, like me, went to Louisiana after Katrina and Rita to provide care to the needy.

The members of my Katrina team:
Dawn Beatty; Andrew Bock; Nancy Detweiler; Cathy Farell; Monty Johnson; Nancy Johnson; Debi Jordan; Rose Marie Nunez; Sue Strong; Jan Theis; Neal Tepper & Jennifer Alexander.

My Arcadian friends
Andrea and Jim McFaul and Angela St.Dizier of the local Mental Health system.
Our gracious hosts in Lafayette
And others who had influenced me along the way…..
Special thanks and acknowledgements to

The Dixie Chicks
and

Benny Andersson, Tim Rice and Bjorn Ulvaeus for their inspirational songs.

The Wrath and fury of nature

HOLY BEACH, LA 2005 (After the Hurricane Rita).

MAP OF LOUISIANA

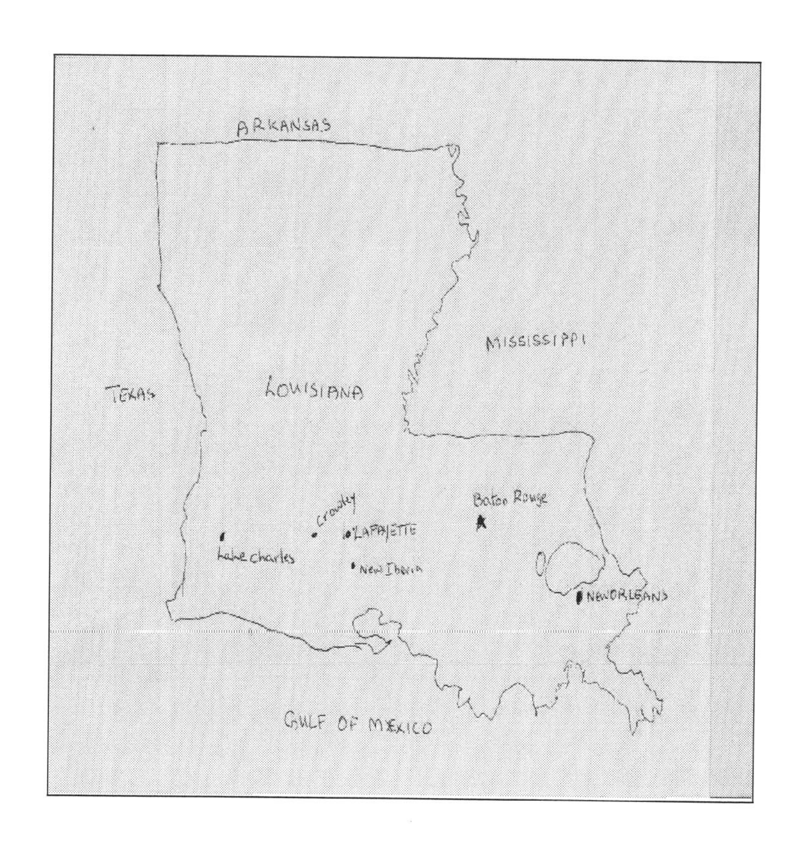

HURRICANES

KATRINA

AUGUST, 29 2005.
Deaths 1836.

RITA

SEPTEMBER, 24 2005.
Deaths 119.

PREFACE

My lifelong friend, Dr Kattuman, is a "professor of economics" at Cambridge.

Paul is also an exquisite word -smith.

His pecuniary repertoire, though immense, seldom unsettle me. I fancy myself, to stand, toe to toe, in the reflecting pools of our intellectual ambiance.

The world of Words renders a different story, from the days, when Mr. PremChandran, our English teacher, taught us Shakespeare in grade school, Paul stood, a Hercules, towering over my literary skills. Sentences used to cascade from his pen with scintillating brilliance.

Thirty years later, we met again at Cambridge, and I held him in the same awe as I did three decades ago.

Our conversation shied away from money and human psyche.

That crisp English evening, we kept Virgil over a glass or two of Paul's collection of single malts. We talked about the good old days of our adolescence, when we sang and danced to Mary Hopkins's "Those were the days".

Paul and I shared a bond that kept us linked forever.

The two of us, along with other notables, had spent about 8 years in a boarding school, joining the institution as 9 year olds.

Sainik School Kazhakootam is one among the many military schools in India. The brainchild of the Defense Minister, the venerable visionary, Mr. VK Krishna Menon, these educational crucibles had a philosophical bend towards the famous Eaton of England.

SSKZM could not boast of a Lord Willington, William Pitt, Thomas Gray, PB Shelly, George Orwell, Princes William and Harry, Premier Cameron, Ian Flaming, or a James Bond, but my alma mater would reach similar heights and fame as the cradle that raised many an important Indian.

Eaton had quite a handsome head start over SSKZM since the inception in 1440 by the King of England.

We were the class of '75.

Dispersed to four corners of the world, we remained connected through the e mail group. The absence of constant communication did not in any way adulterate our bond. Never being a fan of the twitter culture, where people are driven by their narcissistic Id to exhibit every second of their lives and in return be gratified by its voyeuristic appeal, I did not have the compulsion or desire to know everything but just the important things.

We talked about the current state of our friends making the customary walk down the memory lane of roll numbers.

Starting with 621.....

In Paul's own words "Thinking back all the way to
Our beginnings, to the bunch of unprepossessing, scrawny and callow
Juveniles from over four decades ago! Gosh! We did not knowingly spare anyone of course. Things were not all rosy then, and not now, nor ever, but do you know, we felt just deeply, profoundly, thankful that the specific bunch that are us, through sheer randomness of chance, had the opportunity to share lives then, warts and all, and even more, share our lives at least a little, now.

As a group we can not only weather, but should indeed be thankful for, a little misunderstanding, a bit of bickering, a spot of grandstanding, and smidgeon of hyperbole and so on, all part of the recipe. As a family, we are more functional than most families I know!"

(I am quoting Paul, to give a glimpse and taste of his flavorful literary might.)

That evening was reserved for us to remise those giddy days.
All of us had our favorite heroes among the teachers.

The most popular ones, NBN, Prem Chandran, CG George and the Sharmas had their ardent followers.

My hero was the Principal, Wing commander Roy. He made me think outside the box, teaching me to lead and not be lead. This man supported me through the painful days when I transformed myself from being a soldier to a doctor.

Though not very popular with the staff, Roy, who adored a special place in our hearts, turned out to be just an extraordinary person, quite different from his predecessor, the doughy Commander GD Singh.

Many an evening, he drove from house to house, collecting the senior students like the pied piper with his enchanting music ,enticing us all, to his quarters. From the dormitories, in darkness of night, sped the black

Ambassador car. Even in the clutches of inebriation, he had a firm grip on the road. Princi, our impeccable hero could do no wrong. We were drunk with the innocence of youth.

We partied at his house. He considered us his students, family and friends, all rolled into one.
He was always smashed with rum and coke while we indulged in limeade. The drinks were served by his "Gurkha batman", prim and proper in beautiful cocktail glasses with the red cherry and all.

We talked about how wonderful an anglophile, Wing Commander Roy, was.

We chatted away into the early hours of the morning, the two of us and the bottle of Single malt.

I did not mention my yearning to Paul, my literary ambition to write a novel that would make him proud.

In the late forties, the impending "mid- life crisis" culminated in my Acadian trip.
The consequence of this odyssey was my new found passion for disaster psychiatry.

My secret desire and nascent passion colluded to make my pipe dream a reality.

Moved by the experience in Louisiana, I tried to raise the awareness, in the community, as well in my social and academic circles, about the plight of that state's schools. I wrote to the school board. The creative e mail list included our parish priest and everyone else on the Roman Catholic ladder, all the way up to the Pope.

Letters flew to many others in high places.

The pleading and cajoling letter sounded something like this.......

Dear friend,

I am Dr. N.J. Jacob, a psychiatrist on the faculty of the University Of Pittsburgh School of medicine. I recently had the opportunity to go and work with the people of Southern Louisiana following the two hurricanes, Katrina and Rita. The super storms caused wide spread devastation in the states of Louisiana, Mississippi, Alabama and Texas. My volunteer work was in the state of Louisiana and hence the exposure and experience was limited to the same. The extent and intensity of destruction was mind- numbing.

Our team of volunteers consisting of therapists, nurse, social workers, psychologist and psychiatrist, through SAMHSA (Substance Abuse and mental Health Services

Administration) provided behavioral healthcare to hundreds of people.

One of the most heart-breaking effects of the hurricanes is the damage and or destruction of up to 70% of schools along the southern coast of Louisiana.
I write this letter, requesting you to open your heart and help those proud “Cajuns” who will not seek charity.

I know most of you have already given in abundance...

However, the world has moved on to more glamorous news and calamities. The victims or the destruction are no longer on the TV and they hardly get any mention at all. But months after Katrina and Rita, people remain crushed. A long and difficult road to recovery awaits those residents. This would take years and collective efforts from all of us Americans. The state of Louisiana is in economic ruin and the most vulnerable are the children.

Please think about adopting a school in Louisiana in some form. The extent of the relationship with any of the schools is up to you and your organization. I am not advocating a one-time huge capital expenditure, rather a long -term investment in the future of those precious children.

My 14 year old daughter pitched the case to her school board on my behalf and she aptly said:
"Help them now and these students will be contributing citizens of the future. Ignore them and they would become the inevitable burden to society.”

You can obtain the name of a school and contact person, usually the Principal or board secretary, from the Louisiana

schools web- site.
http://www.louisianaschools.net/lde/index.html
Some of the worst hit areas are New Orleans, St. Bernard, Vermillion, Cameron and Lake Charles.

My life has changed dramatically since the visit. I have no personal monetary interest in making this connection between you and those of southern Louisiana. But believe me, immense and intangible gratification is a sure bet to get this project through. Attached please find a few photographs to give you insight into the extent of misery in Louisiana.

Sincerely,
………

Sad but true, this was a pathetic letter.

I did not get any takers among the Pope, the governor, the parish or my children's school board.

I did not expect any response from the governor or the Pope of course.

The Parish priest and the designate from the Pittsburgh diocese were kind enough to write me letters with accompanying blessings. The school board had money for larger stadiums but none for these kids.

Back at the University, I spoke to the psychiatry residents with lots of fire and brimstone in my oration. Many of them wanted to go down to LA, but the passions that would have launched a thousand dreams of idealism met premature deaths at the bosom of bureaucratic mediocrity.

In May of 2006 I returned to Louisiana with Dr. Umapathy as invitees of the federal government. He had made a similar trip to New Orleans.

I staggered along the infamous Bourbon Street that looked like a virgin, unmolested by the hurricane.

And

I tiptoed through the lower ninth ward still reeking of stench and reeling in its depravity.

The two icons were just the same as before; nothing had really changed!
It was a contrast on different planes of lassitude.

Needless to say, I was a changed man.
That short sojourn in the swamps of the rustic south had altered my life forever. Gone was the turpitude of Middle class American complacence.

To quill the restlessness, I took up the challenge of the schizophrenia unit, the most challenging one at WPIC. Friends analyzed it as self flagellation, jokingly comparing me with the Albino Opus Di member in "Da Vinci Code."

I even changed jobs to join the VA, to care for the returning veterans of the Iraq and the Afghanistan wars. The stories they told were quietly locked away in the dungeons of hypocrisy. The air in that dark place got too toxic for me over time and I escaped back to the safety of the citadel.

Three years since I started talking about the devastating effects of the Gulf Coast hurricanes of 2005, I was still preaching to deaf ears.

I finally got tired of hearing my own voice as it swam against the tide, to keep afloat over the cacophony of sexier tunes. The bells tolled for melodrama, and the cheers echoed the beating of war drums. The soul and mind, faced with repeated assault on humanity, had become a cauldron of hopelessness.

Then an idea began to take shape.....

I should let my fantasy garnish a life of its own and set my imagination free.

Why not write a story, yes write someone else's story.......?

Maybe this story would make, an interesting coffee table companion, for all the people who live the lie and scurry away from the truth, and for all those who find solace in myths, so seamlessly propagated by the media.

In the following months, in the center of cataclysmic misery, the oasis of dissociation and fictionalization became my beacons of hope.

I set out to create this novel, a story of an incredulous journey… a dream work of my imagination...

It has taken me years to complete this book; not because it was a long epic but I had to tread the waters of my own emotional entanglement to the story.

Here it is, finally, my "Magnum Opus".

Just as in H. W. Longfellow's epic poem Evangeline, this is fiction written on a matrix of loosely woven facts.

Fourteen short days turned out to be a seemingly endless lifetime for three women and two men, strangers brought together by a common calamity...

Five Americans, from their mundane daily lives of stability and superficial tranquility, were quickly taken over by their inherent ambiguity.

The vines of their sorrow, hope, passion and despair rapidly entwined with those of the people of Acadiana.

Their lives were changed forever.

Many of you, when told about my grandiose vision of writing this novel, had expectations of a quasi academic work about the human experience , endurance and suffering in the aftermath of Katrina and Rita seen through my psychiatrist's eyes . Though there are horrifying stories told with a blend of reality and fiction, I will not trivialize or sully the memories of the enormous pain of people of Louisiana. This Novel is in a lighter vein and is written about human drama, just some intriguing melodrama!

Characters

Players

Walter Higgin, MD.
Jill Perkins, MD.
Tammy Peters MSW.
Brian Hodge, PHD.
Paul Maslin LSW, MBA.
Joanne Cuff, B Sc, RN.

Andrea and Jim Le Blanc and Angela of the Lafayette mental health team.
Mary and John Pellerin the hosts.
Tom Peters/Denis Cormier men in Tammy's life.
SAMHSA doctor Dr. Hesston.
Mr. Watson of FEMA

Cynthia McAlister, MD chief resident.
Drs. Adele, Mary, Rob, Rick, and Eric.

Dawn, Andrew, Neil, Dr Golden, Cathy, Nancy, Monty, Debi, Rose Marie, Jan and Jennifer.

Patients

Mindy:	"The borderline".
Ken :	"The sociopath".
Luke:	Vietnam vet with PTSD.
Mark:	Vietnam vet with PTSD.
Jules:	"The hit man".
Vanessa:	The elderly woman looking for her grandson.

Davis:	The NOLA police officer.
Jennifer:	Young lady with eating Disorder.
JC:	Bipolar.
Jim:	National guardsman.
Bill :	National guardsman.
Tanya:	The Social worker with daughter Monica.
John Doe:	The demented man.
Mike:	The homeless.
Jenna	Soldier with MST.

Tim/Tiffany.
Mary and patches.

Unnamed man in the jail.
Unnamed couple.
Unnamed drug addict.
Unnamed homeless schizophrenic.

PROLOGUE

January 29, 2006

*I*t was another cold January night in Pittsburgh. The freezing rain air brushed Gaelic texture to the mystic misery that hung around like the London fog. The fragrance of doom permeating the atmosphere was a harbinger of events to come. The winter was gentle until last week. Crocus with their purple, violet, blue and even crimson hues had popped up in the back yard, conned into an exuberance of early spring while snow drops craved the comforting blanket of continued frosty whiteness. They added contrast to the green grass that failed to die brown this winter. People talked about global warming but the weather remained just small talk for most except Al Gore.

Dr. Walter Higgin was driving home in his old SUV. The "socialist" came with a few idiosyncratic capitalist facets, a fact, his uber conservative friend Adele, promptly pointed out. One among them was the German motor vehicle, he self mockingly, called his Nazi wheels. He always blamed the "Pittbughese" topography for having forced the gas guzzler upon him many miles ago. He often promised his bleeding heart he would buy a cheaper and greener form of transportation the next time around.

Truth be told, at one stage in his life, Walter had craved an expensive one. He had set his heart on a Porsche Boxter but had to settle for the Mercedes M class. His wife vetoed the sexy Boxter as a chick magnet. Albeit it's sexiness, he still basked in the expression of admiration or envy, whenever he majestically disembarked from this boxy, engineering marvel.

He adored it several years ago. At the present time, it was, the remnant of a whimsical fancy, like the once shinny armor of this now pasty weather beaten car, just a distant juvenile dream.

They ceased to be extensions of his ego.

Dr.Higgin's career at the ivory towers of psychiatry had been on auto pilot. He found a cliché in the maze of academia as a clinician educator, an excellent one and well liked by the students for his bedside teaching.
Walter cloistered over 12 years. He won many accolades including the physician of the year once and couple of Golden Apple awards for best teacher. Mary, his mentor plodded him to explore the teacher clinician track for promotion but he never wanted to venture outside the comfort zone.

His students, residents and fellows constituted his pride and joy. He taught, trained and inspired many young physicians over the years. Stellar performers lit up the sky. Dr. Jill Perkins, a junior faculty at WPIC, unequivocally became the darling of his eyes. He had known Jill for some time now. He claimed to be her mentor through her medical school, residency, and fellowship. Today she had become his colleague. A delectable camaraderie existed between them. Though diametrically opposite in many ways, they subscribed to an intangible alliance. Most importantly they enjoyed each other's company.

Dr. Higgins had it all, a wonderful family, lots of friends, adoring students, rewarding job, big house, luxury cars, plenty of money and a rejuvenated body……

Yes, Dr. Walter Higgin had attained the American dream. He should be on cruise control for another 20 years and then ride away into the sunset of retirement.

Yet sadly he remained a troubled soul. He appeared to be searching for the Holy Grail, the ambrosia of tranquility amidst the wilderness of emptiness.

The winding northward Route 8 from the downtown Pittsburgh to the rural heartland of Butler endured loneliness except for a few rich suburbanites in their Escalades and Beamers returning possibly from a ballet at the cultural district.

Walter gazed at the dark endless path before him, despising the truth. This route had come to symbolize his life, empty san a few bright flickering lights.

These specks of happiness included his frequent discussions with Eric, Rob, Rick and Adele.

Eric the nonchalant liberal; Rob, the consummate consensus builder and Adele perched right off Ann Coulter.

Eric tutored Walt on world politics. Astute and knowledgeable, he had an insider track into the corridors of power. Nothing rattled Eric. He had an aura of intellectual detachment which he used to shield against the pains of daily living.

Rob, did the objectivity exercise ad nauseaum, reluctant to take a definite stand in the political divide. In the crunch time, he did what many of us only talked about .....He went were most of us will never dare to go.

Walt had all but given up the war of the words with Adele because he finally realized the futility.

Rick and he wasted away long hours of mental masturbation on any topic they chanced upon.

Much water had flown under the bridge in the last few seasons....
An undeclared war of cultures raged over the world with thousands caught in the cross wires of religious, ethnic, and financial cleansing.

People, more than ever before, slipped into the chasm of economic slavery.

His brain survived two elections.
The soul had gone through years of tragedies.
His body fought against diseases and won battles in eyes of others.
Jill had fallen in love with Dr. Tomlinson, a surgeon and Walter had felt pangs of envy.

Dr. Higgin appeared to have emerged stronger from those escapades. He had shed a few pounds and got in to the act of running. He enjoyed jogging 10K three or four times a week and loved the endorphin rush. Walter ran around the picturesque North Park Lake, a 5 mile track. Adding a loop at the boat house and along the public tennis courts made it an even 10K. For him this amounted to a mind cleansing run.

These beautiful Pittsburgh spring, summer or fall evenings were his soothing companions.
He ran the great race two years in a row.

All that bravado was just a façade camouflaging the raging existential crisis.

He continued to sink deeper and deeper……
The deafening silence of dearth failed to be muffled by the peatiness of Islay single malt.

He longed for those days at the thatched cottage atop the cliff in Oban where he sat gazing at the enchanting Islay across the Sound of Kerrera. The chaffing winds caressing his cheek, salty spray tearing his eyes, the scent of the rotting seaweeds dancing at his nostrils, and a dram of "usquebaugh", the water of life, blazing a path of warmth for his wretched soul….a virtual escape to weekends in Scotland.

In the stillness of the night, the song "Someone else's story" sung by Helen Sjooholm drifted by over the drone of the speeding car.

His favorite song from the musical Chess, though "Latin" to him rendered in Swedish, was so powerful and heart wrenching.

Walter felt "Florence's" chords of agony with each note….

He knew the English lyrics quite well and he hummed those words connecting with the melody in Swedish.

The words haunted him…..

Last year…..

The year 2005 was one of damnation.

Dr Higgins reflected on Jill, his protégée.

Recently, more than ever, his intrusive thoughts had been full of her.

Walt watched a phantasmagoria of her short life, her beautiful mind and youthful body over and over.

Did he attempt to lead a life of adventure voyeuristically through that of Jill?

He had encouraged Jill to explore her inner self. It was her life and not his to play Russian roulette with!

His mind ruminated forever.

"Why was I so naive? If only I had been more candid with her."

"She was so strong, if only she had been more open."

"Even she was fooling herself and if only, she was not so good at it."

"She minimized it."

"She hid it from us all."

"I was not objective. I was blinded by her dazzling personality."

"One time I should have been accurate in the assessment of emotionality, I was so wrong"

The "If only undoing game" plagued his soul and mind.

The darkness of the starless Pittsburgh sky flowed into the deepest abysm of his shattered soul, reminding him of the futility of his journey.

With a sigh of resignation and acceptance, he pulled over to the empty church parking lot as if the hallowed ground would offer him sanctity.

In the stillness of the lonely night, accentuated by the broodingly somber melody, he saw nothing but the fog, no light at the end of the tunnel.

The walls closed in…

He felt hopeless, helpless and was filled with remorse but without any cognitive dissonance.

He solemnly opened the glove compartment and reached for the....

CHAPTER 1

United States of America

It was the fall of 2005.
The days of dazzling Katrina headlines and kaleidoscopic images in scintillating colors; fragmented tints of racism, poverty, hypocrisy, greed and heroism were fast fading from the collective memory of the nation.

The American public, like a sponge on the autopsy table, had soaked up the last drop of the wall to wall television coverage. Their fervor for vicarious experience of reality easily matched the survivor and American idol of the later years. Such carnivorous voracity had not been noted in the people since the War, The Operation Iraqi Freedom, when they had a glorious treat of an aseptic and morally gratifying gastronomic spectacle of carnage.

This was the ultimate Survivor show!
The thousand plus dead and hapless souls, in their macabre watery graves, drowned again in the geyser of rabidly frothing, pontificating self righteous proclamation of self fulfilling prophecy.

The mundane truths of the American Pompeii fought a lackadaisical battle against the apocalyptic myths spewing from Mount Vesuvius of mainstream media.

The feverish news cycles with sprinkling of spectacular rescues conveniently evaded the frigid decomposing bodies.

The Interstate 10 overpass, submerged under gushing waters, was a bridge to nowhere..........
It became the epitome of a hundred thousand people with no place to go, the quintessence of modern day slavery.

The black "looter" and the white "survivor", they both swam to stay afloat and alive. The human suffering and misery brought out the worst in fellow brothers. Kane and Abel fought all over again.

The smug dwarfs of officialdom patted each other's backs.
"One heck of a job Brownie"
"Yes quite a bang up effort indeed!"

The sexy media handlers in their crisp designer digs and chalky makeup milked the tragedy. People marveled at the courage of the TV Heroes who braved the nature and the rule of the jungle to go where no official could or would enter. They became instant celebrities and cranked out their own telecast shows on return to civilization.

An odd American wondered how the news crew managed to get there when the mighty government convoy did not.

The shell shocked America appeared worse than a ravaged Africa!

The president speaking, at the Jackson square, illuminated by eerie blue light reflecting off St. Paul's Cathedral, sported a cadaveric expression While the 90 year old at the convention center, slumped dead in her wheel chair, looked angelically alive, two portraits of American tragedy, sharing a somber resemblance.

The elderly woman, with unruly silvery stands of hair and a face gorged deep by rivers of sorrow sat cloaked in the national banner of the country that had send her son to Vietnam. Tours later, he has returned in a coffin draped in the American flag.

Decades ago, lying in the waterlogged paddy fields half a world away, wounded bleeding and dying, he was waiting for the medevac chopper that never came. Today, she too would wait for the same sound of rescue, still covered in red white and blue, the flag that the Marine Corps had presented her after her son's burial at Arlington.

Her husband, a buffalo soldier, shed his last drop of blood for his country in the frigid European winter during WWII.

The 11 year old, dressed in shorts and flowery tee shirt, laid face down and dead, floating in the murky water. The other day she was shooting hoops in the hood. Maybe one day she would have become a star. A basketball player who might have brought glory to her country.

The 4 year old's body lay crumbled in a tiny heap of rotting human flesh covered with a tarp to keep away the hungry dogs.

Soldiers in their battle fatigues and classy shades marched in formation. Never missing a step and oblivious to the forgotten dead between orange traffic cones.

The world looked on in bewildered disbelief at the heart wrenching pictures of the American Tsunami, snap shots of torrid, ravished, and "swept under "capitalistic poverty.

Alas and so predictably,

They quietly slipped into to the comfort of the inner pages. Those caricatures began their metamorphosis into banished footnotes in the history of the richest country.

Rita, another one of those super Atlantic hurricanes, rolled in a month later heading for the western part of Louisiana and eastern Texas.

The smurfs of power, not to be caught with their pants down this time around, set in to motion, a grandiose evacuation plan that was outshone only by their lack of understanding of human nature.

The wheels of anticipation turned feverishly. The media took up position to provide the country a sky box view. Suffering had become a spectator sports extravaganza.

Rita delivered less destruction compared to Katrina in terms of the death toll. But inevitably, it showcased authorities, with the same enormity of ineptness.

There were many fund raisings, out pouring of sympathy, money, hands and goods from the Good Samaritan populace of the world.

The governments, politicos and pundits haggled over infinitesimal points and continued their projective identification of negligence and incredulous incompetence.

But soon…

As the brackish waters engulfing the poorer parishes and wards of New Orleans receded, leaving behind goulash streaks of death and mayhem, King George and the knights of the main stream media galloped off to greener pastures of sensationalism. The destruction of the natural's fury was outdone only by the priapisamic impotence of the administrations at all levels.

The front pages reverted back to moronic news bits. Sports events replaced the gory picture of destruction. The color of dark grief turned into glitter of gold and green for the main street America while the streets of New Orleans continued to be carpeted with industrial slime, human and animal excreta, ghastly mould and tons of thrash.

The country had moved on….

Yet there were many Americans who were heart broken by the suffering of their brethrens.
They were waiting in the wings, to be called up to do their bit, as they went about with mundane daily rigmarole.

Many of them would soon embark on a journey of their life time….

CHAPTER 2

DAY ONE

PITTSBURGH, PENNSYLVANIA

Tuned to 88.3 FM, she was listening to Studs Terkel, social historian, radio host and Pulitzer Prize winning author on Emmy Goodman's Democracy Now.

The conversation centered on President Bush, Mahalia Jackson, James Baldwin, Louis Armstrong and New Orleans.

Terkel, who prided himself as the "Guerrilla journalist with a tape recorder" showed praises on Emmy.

He called her part of the prescient minority, the prophetic minority. that stood up against injustice during the history of this country.

He kept going and the interview in the fire house grinded on.

A liberal talk show still drew a blush, highlighting the cheek bones of her chiseled face.

Not too long ago she was an ardent fan of the other end of the broad band. She had not forgiven her to have let herself be duped for so long ….like many other egocentric compatriots of hers.

She realized that sometimes it warranted a personal tragedy, to tear away the blinders we adorned to protect us from visualizing the painful truth. And even then, powerful forces worked perpetually to alter our perception of reality. Gratified with faux knowledge, spoon fed to us in colossal proportions, we clung to the most dogmatic and twisted rationale contorting the truth.

Pittsburgh is an almost unique city but is a bit like San Francisco. Imagine identical topography with the roller coaster roads and add ice and snow to the inclines. Hills stockade the city in the river valley. East had the confluence of three rivers; the Allegheny and Monongahela Rivers forming the Ohio River at the Point with its Geyser in lieu of the Bay in the west. Provincial townships nestled in the terraced hillsides. The houses were salt boxes unlike the mission adobes.

Six hundred communities made up the metropolis.
For years the city had a bad rap of being the sooty sunless Steel City, polluted and with skyline that was invisible on the sunniest day because of the haze around the mills.

The seventies witnessed the economic distress of closing steel mills and the eighties ushered in the renaissance.

The modern Pittsburgh replaced the dingy dust covered row houses and marched into the Forbes magazine as one of the best places in the country to live in the Nineties and beyond.

Oakland was a city in itself. The Pitt, Carnegie Mellon and Carlow universities, Presbyterian, Children's, Montifore , Western Psych and Magee hospitals and the Peterson event center sitting at the top of the hill, made Oakland the heart of urban academic and health scene.

The fall was still in the pangs of a dying summer and Jill had quite a pleasant haul from Shadyside to Oakland. Leaves, yellow, orange and red from the oak, maple and walnut trees lining the windswept street littered the dark tarmac. Many of them were very old, as old as the buildings of Oakland. She always admired the majestic monuments forming an envious collection of jewels on the architectural crown of this University City.

She glimpsed the Cathedral of Learning a street over. This Basilica of the University of Pittsburgh, towering over all, like a huge candle, stood on an expanse of green between the Forbes and the Fifth avenues. The plush lawns, covered with early morning dew, seemed devoid of life at this time of the morning. This would change dramatically as the day unfolded. In a corner of the greenery, shaded by the shadow of the cathedral, was the serene Heinz chapel.

A sigh escaped her. And a tear rolled down her cheek.

Mike and she had planned to get married at the Chapel one day.

Her friend and co resident Dan had his wedding there. It was a marvelous ceremony she and Dr Higgin attended a few years ago.

She was single, young and a resident then.

Walter led her to the Pittsburgh Athletic club for the reception across the street, the club was an architectural reminiscent of the 16th century Grimani Palace in Venice and stood a small walk from the Heinz chapel.

"I want to get married at this chapel" Jill remarked, still mesmerized by the magical glow of the chapel.
"I will give you away if your father is not available, besides you need to find a man."
It was a private joke between the two because Jill had problems with steady dates.

"Maybe I will marry you." Jill chided. She had the mischievous glint in her eyes.

"Ah I would have to get divorced first." Walter replied with his accompanying laughter.

Seasons later, Jill met Mike Tomlinson, a surgeon and a Captain in the reserves. It was love at first sight.

Last spring Jill and Mike had walked along the winding road under the green shady oak and maple trees. Flowers in their glorious bloom, lined the gravel path. Majestic tulips in the cool Pittsburgh breeze appeared as cascades of rainbows.

Time flew by and last winter became a sheet of stark despair. She had watched, helplessly, as the pandemonium unfolded during that fateful weekend.

The men and women in immaculate ceremonial uniforms....
The smart salutations, gleaming swords and gun salutes....

A lone bugler played the "TAPS".

The haunting melody and lyrics of the civil war song would, be forever, etched in her memory.

And afterwards, the people trooped past in respect.

She heard the familiar "I am so sorry for your loss. He was a hero......" Those hollow sentences of sympathy would later echo in the caves of loneliness.

Ah.....Every bit was a blur with such clarity, played over and over in slow motion.

Captain Mike Tomlinson was country's offertory to the scorching sands of Iraq.
He laid down his life, trying to save lives of others, patching up IED devoured limbs of nineteen year olds.

In the unrelenting cold vastness of those cruel dawns, eerily silent and devoid of the cooing of the coffee machine, she lay awake. Her nostrils clamored for the wisp aroma of the savory decoction.

Jill missed the radiant warmth and the strong arm around her slender waist. She yearned for those lazy Sunday mornings when rays of sunshine crept through the blinds to wake them both.

Mike rapidly became yet another name, just a number, carved in the totem pole of iconic folklore, soon to be relegated to the realms of a relic collecting dust.

Even the microcosm of Oakland had forgotten the homegrown hero.

Winds of time swept away the last trace of valor and she became the lone sentinel on the sandy dunes of memory.

For Jill, the torture was just beginning.

Serpents replaced the numbness and the loneliness in her life.

She woke up in cold sweat all most every night.

Her cotton nightgown, drenched in briny clammy sweat and clinging to her bosom, sent shivers through her body.

Her heart was pounding against her breasts. She had choking and drowning sensations. She heard her own raspy breathing.

Thrashing and fighting the unknown demons, she was experiencing yet another nightmare.

Night after night…..

They came back to haunt her, twice or three times on some dreary nights.

The sequence of daunting terror always presented the same scenario.

The curtain opened with Jill and Mike in London.

It was the nonnegotiable spot for their honeymoon.

The British capitol was Jill's favorite stomping ground. London had been the launching pad for her annual European safari. They always used the tube as their mode of transportation, to transverse the city, free from the tangles of the traffic quagmire aboveground.

A Shakespearian buff to the core, she never missed a chance to catch a play at the Globe theatre along the banks of the winding Themes. She preferred the open-air yard ling seating. She braved the London rain for hours to watch the thespian masterpiece of the Bard of Avon every time they were in London.

That morning they started their walk from Copthorne Tara hotel on Scar dale Place, a stone throw away from High

Street Kensington through the streets of Knightsbridge to the Harrods. After some window shopping, they brought scones, tarts and steaming coffee for their breakfast. Back on the streets, they walked through Kensington garden and to Hyde Park, basking in the crisp London sun, enjoying the English delicacies. They jumped on the tube at Hyde Park Corner to ride their favorite subway, the Piccadilly line.

After stop at Green Park the train stopped at Piccadilly Circus. This is where they would get off the Piccadilly line to take the Bakerloo line towards the Globe. But that would be this evening. They had two tickets for the 730 PM Tempest tonight.

They went past Covenant gardens. Jill loved the festive atmosphere of the market. Mike always enjoyed the fish and chips made by the Venetian chef at the English stall run by the Sikh.

They would visit the Gardens on their return.

As the train slowed and then stopped at Kings Cross station, the doors flung open and a dozen demonic middle easterners in their long white robes and checkered turbans jumped Mike. Sitting on him, they shouted into the walkie-talkie in crisp English accent learned only in the playing fields of Eaton.

"Yes we got him he is our man, our terrorist"

"Jolly Good show old chap"

They fired in unison a thousand shots, bursting his head into a million pieces.

Jill's outstretched hands felt the viscous splatter of blood that was, warm, turbid and hotter than the summer sun in the Mesopotamian desert.

She woke up!

Night after night this sequence continued to molest her mind.
As a psychiatrist, she had very little interest in dreams. They held no significance to her except for the dance of neurotransmitters in REM sleep.

But these nightmares were tearing her apart.

Bicycles in Oakland are not that rare but they are nothing like those in Manhattan. The drivers, over the years, had come to accept them and learned to coexist. She had a flat stretch; a premium in Pittsburgh. Jill lived in one of the charming row houses, old yet each one with a story to tell. Many of the faculty owned them and the rows had an academic culture to it. The students occupied the less attractive apartments.
A curious yet subtle pecking order ran through the veins of this neighborhood.

Born in the homogenous heartland of Pennsylvania farm country, Jill grew up conservative in a Christian household.

Her older brother joined the Marines to become decorated veteran and the pride of the family. Her father, an army vet, who lost a leg in the rice fields of Nam, was reduced to the role of a washed out junkie in a wheel chair. She wanted to follow in their footsteps and was planning to be a sailor. But in her college years she ran away from the killing fields to saving lives. She still held on to her conservative thinking.

She was always clear about her life and goals.

Go to University of Pittsburgh for under graduate college. That would be her first time away from home and living alone.

She hoped to do medical school and residency also at Pitt. She did not want to be too far from home.

After a surgery residency, she would get married, raise a family, have career and then ride off into the golden sunset of retirement.

But,

In the third year of medical school, she met a crazy professor who convinced her that there was no better adventure than psychiatry, the voyage into the souls of humanity. Something the men of cloak would heatedly contest. She blossomed into a fine psychiatrist and joined one of the finest institutions of the land.

She had a luncheon date with him today. She always felt a tingle of excitement with Dr. Higgin. Her physical reaction to his presence always surprised her. She ambiguously delighted in Walter's admiring eyes as they feasted on the curvy smoothness and sensuality of her womanhood.

She rode by the empty Syria lot, soon it would be full. That's where most of the junior faculty and the residents parked. She passed the "Soldiers and Sailors", a monumental work of architecture. , It always provoked a sense of awe in her. She glanced along Thackeray Street looking for Mr. Singh's food truck. His Mutton Biriyani was delicious but today, she would most likely eat at Peter's Pub with Dr. Higgin.

Oakland was bustling with the usual morning crowd.

Dr Perkins is not a fitness freak but she loved to keep healthy and a trim sexy figure gave her a good bargain for her efforts. She is about 5' 7" and a size 2 exploited her natural curves, a perfect 34 c.
She liked wearing dark turtle necks that cuddled her perky firm breasts. Her blond hair she kept long and her eyes were a pair of sparkling turquoise sea. A slim waist and shapely tall legs carried her figure so well. She did turn a few heads in the big house.

Though she was a member of the faculty, many a students, residents and fellow faculty cast admiring glances at her. She was quite aware of the lusting eyes and enjoyed the attention that her seductive body brought her. She was not shy of her sexuality.
She had a bubbly personality to go along with her physical attractiveness though it came with some caustic edges.

Her 21 speed roadster raced up the O' Hara street past the engineering and Research buildings to the corner of Desoto and O'Hara where the Big house stood. Turning right, she made her way into the J parking Lot, the most coveted real estate in Oakland. Though she was a junior faculty and did not have the privilege of the seniors to earn a parking spot, she parked her bike between the pillars. In winter as the weather got chilly she took the bus. She did not own a car after her old corolla died.

She was starting yet another day in the hospital. The big house had become her asylum from the haunting past and the daunting demons of her future.

Steps led from the garage to the main hospital through carded doors.
Midway through her climb her cell phone went off.

"Hi, this is Dr Perkins"
"Hello, Dr Perkins. Dr. Hesston here. How are you doing today? Are you ready for some adventure?" A raspy voice commented from the other end.

She did not know any Dr Hesston.
"I am sorry; I should have mentioned I am representing SAMHSA." Dr Hesston chuckled.

"Oh, SAMHSA! Yes Dr. Hesston " Jill was excited.

She knew that SAMHSA is the acronym for Substance Abuse and Mental Health Services Administration. It is the federal body that over sees all the efforts in those two fields.

In the heightened frenzy following the hurricanes of the gulf coast, Jill had put her name in every the possible list of volunteers, from APA to FEMA to Red Cross, and had forgotten all about it in her busy daily life. Now they sought her expertise. They wanted her to go down to Louisiana to work as a disaster psychiatrist for two weeks.

"We don't have anyone in Lafayette. I want you to lead a team there; can you be there on the ground in forty eight hours?"

The sudden turn of events transfixed Jill. She had not done anything like this before.

Images of the superdome flashed through her mind and her heart began to pound...

She felt warm purple blood splattered on her face. She heard Mike choking in the brackish waters of the lower ninth with Marine one flying over and the president's mouth forming inaudible words. Everything drowning in the thunderous sound of the Piccadilly Circle metro......

"Dr Perkins are you there?" Dr Hesston said with some concern in a southern drawl.

It brought Jill back to reality....

“Yes I am here, yes I can do that”
“Well that’s settled I will see you soon. Good luck Jill.” she signed off.

Dr. Perkins started her mental speed dial.
She had to find Lafayette on a map first.

She was ticking off all the things she needed to do before she embarked on this trip.

Clinical coverage.
Week end call.
Malpractice.
Travel arrangements.
Packing…..

She did harbor a nagging fear though all this commotion.
"What about those nightmares?"

“Well, I will handle them”

Before long…..

Day one would be upon them and she would be flying to her Odyssey.

She did not have the slightest idea what was waiting for her in the Bayous of Louisiana.

CHAPTER 3

Day one

Tallahassee, Florida

Juan Ponce de León the Conquistador from Spain searched for gold and the fountain of youth.
He, in his prior sailing, had conquered Dominican Republic and Puerto Rico. In 1513, on landing in what is now called St Augustine, he called that area la Florida or the land of flowers.
Tallahassee is seated in the Leon County named after him.

Tallahassee, Florida is similar to many other state capitals.

State workers and the "Seminoles" make up the bulk of its population. In spite of the University City label, it was very much a "deep south" city. Steeped in the history of the "plantation past", people called it LA or Lower Alabama.

Under the modern facade lay the lazy times of mint Juleps and Sunday afternoon picnics. It also reverberated of collard greens, hog feet and chicken coops. The Spanish moss hung as garlands of death from live oaks along the roads and the mangrove in the lakes showed off their ugly knees. The life stood still for them akin to the waters of the swamp. Certainly, not a talisman for the cosmopolitan and touristy paradise Florida had become to the rest of the world, it clearly entertained the dichotomy of Florida.

Tammy had left her ranch house at the corner of Ark low Drive.

They lived in of the older upper middle class neighborhoods. She waved to Mr. Thompson. He always worked in the yard tending to his babies, his banana plants that stood at the enclave of his ranch. Like his wife, the trees seem to be ornamental. They never bore any fruit. But they remained in love for fifty years.
The shamrock street is a lazy winding street that circled the golf course and a development that housed older middle class ranch houses in its outer rim. Built in the sixties and seventies, many of them had retirees while the rest served as the adobes of the next generation with small children.

The inner rim had the golf course, and peppering of "on the green"; multi garbled mini palaces .Quite often a hole in one putt landed in the kitchen sink through the picturesque windows.

The inner rim had petite sidewalks where the women walked their dogs in the morning. Tammy, during her morning jogs, ran into some of those desperate housewives clad in bulging leotards, on their power walks. They had a 5lbs dumbbell in one hand a poop bag and a leash in the other. Most nights they slept alone in their king sized beds between soft silk sheets while their business executive husbands spent lonely nights in some far away Marriott.

Shamrock Street turned into Killarney way before joining the Thomasville road.

Thomasville road north, or route 319, took you over the Georgia border into Thomasville, GA .On the other side of the road was the Alfred B Malay state gardens surrounding the three Lakes, Hall, Elizabeth and Overstreet.

She drove south, crossing the interstate 10 and on to the main drag that went round the city, called the capital circle. Capital Circle changed directions from NE to SW until she came to the Tallahassee Municipal airport

Tammy's first solo trip, after their marriage a year ago, started today. 25 years old and fresh out of FSU with masters in social work, she had hung the shingles of private practice. She soon realized that it was very hard to start out in the real world. She and Tom had been high school sweet hearts and married a month after her graduation. Tom made good money as an electrician.

Tammy had received her call that morning.
She reached home and could not contain her excitement.

"Tom you would not guess what happened today"

“Well let me guess, you saw a patient?"Mocked Tom.

Tammy threw her bag at him.

“No silly, I got called to go”

Tammy sat on his lap.

“Where are you going?”

Tom put his arm around her waist and pulling her close to him.

“You are not going anywhere”

He laughed and kissed Tammy on her full lips.

Tammy instinctively returned the kiss, her lips pressed against Tom’s.
Tom’s fingers caressed Tammy’s back.
Tammy realized Tom was aroused as she sensed the bulge of his hardness pressing against her behind. Pushing his tongue between her parting lips, Tom sought the moist warmth of her mouth; to taste her tongue and her heat.

Tom palms cupped Tammy’s breast from under.
He groped them through the silky blouse.
Her nipples had grown firm and Tom rolled them between his fingers watching them grow even harder.

She felt his urgency and single-mildness, as he started to tear at her top.

And then her short skirt... they both became a bundle of rags at the foot of the love seat.

Tammy liked soft tender love making. Tom like to control.

It's been the case always. It has only gotten worse since their marriage.
Sex became a power play for Tom. He always wanted to be in control and in his mind his woman obeyed him.

"No" "No" Tammy pleaded as usual.
"No Tom, later~~. Hear what I had to say~~."

"What? I just want you to moan and beg for more"

Tom rolled Tammy over on her back. Lying on the hard cold surface of their Terra cotta floor, the frigidness of the floor hit her naked back and cute ass.
Just the bra and thong prevented total nakedness.

He climbed over her, His weight pinning her down.
She is not petite but Tom is 6feet 6 and 269lbs.
His knee spread her thighs for his fingers to begin his usual caress along the softness of her inner thigh all the way to the edge of her cotton thongs.
Pushing it aside with careless abandon his fingers entered her.

Tammy began to sob.
It was the same story again and again.

"Don't stop crying" Tom barked.

And before she knew it his hardness entered her. It was
tight because she was dry which just excited Tom even
more.
And he started thrusting deep into her.
Tammy could only weep in silence.
This has been the story of her life with Tom.

Well, Tom had been the jock at school, the quarter back
and all. Girls lined up to give him all the blow jobs he
could ask for… Tammy proud to be his girl, and blinded by
that ego trip, neglected herself and ignored the fact that he
was just a predator. Now settled into their married life,
Tom was oblivious to anything being amiss and as usual
was done in 45 seconds flat.
After his orgasm…

He asked lazily "So where are you going to?"

"I am off to Louisiana"

He did not believe her. His little Tammy, she is not going
anywhere he said to himself. Yeah right"

He dismissed her which was worse than the rape he had
just performed……

Later as she lay awake next to snoring Tom, Tammy made up her mind to leave for LA.
She wanted to be respected and not used as an object of someone else's gratification.

She did not want to be a victim anymore.
She will be a savior.
She is going to save lives.

She returned back to earth from her thoughts by the sound of the jet flying over. She had reached the parking lot of the airport. She parked at the long term and taking her luggage from the back, she walked over to the Delta check in.

Soon, she, Tammy Peters was in the air, on her way to Louisiana. Free as a bird or a moth flying towards the candle, to be engulfed in the flames of passion?

CHAPTER 4

DAY ONE

TUSCAN, ARIZONA

Brian did not buy into Dr Hesston's sale pitch about this trip. Waiting to board a flight to Lafayette via Houston the whole exchange upset him and he almost returned home. He lacked the motivation to make the journey to some backward town in Louisiana. The God given mission should have directed him and all his energy to the Crescent city.

New Orleans needed him to do the good Lord's work.

He believed this place was paying for its sins. God showered destruction as punishment for their weakness of the flesh in a city of modern day Sodom and Gomorrah.

He remembered the conference on the weekend of southern decadence.

They stayed at the Sheraton hotel on the canal street. The meeting highlighted Borderline Personality disorders. This affliction fascinated him. Jessie, his last patient with this diagnosis, was as dramatic as they come, carrying arguably the most dreaded label to have in psychiatry. Her rudimentarily formed ego had fostered upon Brian's more mature one to function. Psychiatrists despised this disorder being the hardest to treat. They drained the doctor's self worth and resources. Jessie went from crisis to crisis. She was one of the "hand me down" as she traversed the mental health system. She had burnt all the bridges and had finally ended in Brian's clinic for the poor. Jessie always indulged in self injurious behavior, not necessarily to kill her but to feel the pain. She escaped from the boredom, emptiness and abandonment though cutting herself. Jessie's step father and two stepsiblings had sexually abused her during her preteen years. Her alcoholic mother and her dead beat dad never protected her.

After listening to a lot of heavy stuff, many of his co-conventioneers wanted to spend some relaxing time on the town. A Vieux Carre or French quarter beckoned them in the evening. Brian knew the history of this town. This best known part of the city was founded by a French officer named Bienville.

Brain had foolishly agreed to walk around with others. From Canal Street, the French quarters and the Bourbon Street were only a few streets away.

"That's where all the action is." He overheard his colleagues say with the excitement of high school girls.

On the infamous Street he was repulsed at the sex, vulgarity and intoxication.

"Grown men were on a leash led by scantily clad women, some had the chords around their neck while others had them attached to nipple rings!"
" Males kissed other men publically and women were playing with each other's breasts."
"People lay drunk on the streets in their vomit and urine."

Some of his friends, having imbibed a drink too many, got into the satanic state themselves. They tried to snuggle up to him.
By the end of the night, Brian had thrown up on a side street out of utter revulsion.

In the weeks following Katrina he watched the devil's work on TV.

That was the New Orleans he knew.

He had to go there to be a savior to them.

May be save himself too?

Tucson (Too-Sahn) is an old city engulfed in history of Americans, Mexicans and the Native Americans. Its name comes from the Spanish word O'odham which meant Black base, the volcanic mountains. Tuscan area is a collection of cactus forests and rolling hills.

It is home to the University of AZ. Brian Hodge PhD had obtained his doctorate there. He now taught psychology to the undergrads. He never liked the undergrads, dismissing them as a bunch of unruly juveniles. He had a small house at the fringe of the campus. The school sat at the foothills of Santa Catalina Mountains to the north.

He jumped on a Sun Tran bus en route from the city center to Tucson international airport. He had reservations on the continental flight to Houston.

Brian Hodge was a 40 year old Caucasian. He was single and lived with his mother.

Six feet tall, slim muscular 170 lbs in his wiry frame, he kept his body, the temple of God, in good shape. His dark hair and eyes remained an enigma to Brian. His blonde and blue eyed mother told him stories of his deceased father who looked like Humphrey Bogart in the movie Casablanca.

His parents belonged to the Mennonite Christian sect.

This sect founded by Menno Simons formed part of the peace churches. ~~They stood for non violence, non resistance and pacifism~~. They performed disaster relief services in North America. They still had centers open at Cameron and Hackberry in Louisiana. Brain's father had died in a road accident ~~in Africa~~ while doing missionary work.

The protestant churches moved from the social teaching of Christ to pure biblical inerrancy in the later part of the 20th century and so did Brian. Caught up in the born again movement, he started to, like other evangelicals; believe in salvation attainable only through faith in Jesus and not good work or deeds alone.

He experienced the conversion and an encounter with the power of God to be born again!

The 3rd chapter of Gospel according to John stated.

"The Pharisee Nicodemius came to Jesus admitting that the Galilean in fact was a teacher and sought his advice,
"I tell you no one can enter the kingdom of God without experiencing being born of water and spirit" (john 3.1-5)

Brian was a born again Christian, one among the notables, Jimmy Carter, Bob Dylan and W.

Brian led an exemplary life at least in his mind.
He did not alcohol nor did he smoke or use drugs.
He said grace before each meal.
He strongly believed America to be a Christian Nation .A country that should be governed by born again Christian rules.
He despised the liberals, and the secular people.

In spite of the pious life, Brain was under stress.

Tragic times had begotten Brain. About five weeks ago, Jessie had killed herself by accidental overdose.

Brian had never lost a patient. and he was devastated.

He spend endless nights wondering what if….

"If only I could foresee it happening"
He played it over and over in his mind.

Undoing…..a defense mechanism did not appear to be working for him.

As he climbed on to the plane he wondered "Am I escaping from reality or trying to redeem myself?"

"Is he doing penance for his sins?"

73 or some other random number

CHAPTER ~~5~~

DAY ONE

you are now not even trying to spell things well.

MAPPLEWOOD, MINNISOTA

I love MAPPLE syrup on my pancakes.

-PPAUL

~~Paul~~ Maslin sat at his desk sorting through the weekly team meeting reports resigned to the dull life of pushing papers as an administrator. He and his wife of thirty years had have been their own professional lives. They might as well ~~be~~ on two different planets. Native American affairs occupied her time while Paul immersed himself in his world of providing for the mentally challenged.

the reports were resigned to the dull life.

He was the CEO of ~~a local~~ the St. Paul's programs MH/MR, ~~the community mental health center in St. Paul~~.
They lived in the comfort and quiet of the upscale suburb of Maplewood. AKA Mapplewwwood.

The call to service did not surprise Paul. The very first disaster he was a victim and during the ensuing years he had offered his services at every opportunity.

So when Cain killed Abel, he also damaged Paul. Or maybe Abraham sacrificed PAUL instead of Isaac.

They lived in Grand Forks ND in the spring of 1987.

The Previous autumn brought more than ~~their~~ usual share of rain storms and snow fall about 100 inches. A freak blizzard named Hannah dumped more snow in the first week of April, you know, the fall.

R R F R W

The red river flood of 1997 recorded the worst since the1826. the worst snowfall, I guess.

this happens a lot, I guess, when rivers flood.

The banks overflew into the cities on either side of the border,
Fargo in the USA and Winnipeg in Canada, Grand Forks in ND and East Grand Forks in MN.

there are many national weather services, apparently.

National weather services had predicted a crest level of 49ft which was the height of the dykes. The levees broke flooding the low lying Lincoln Drive neighborhood of Grand Forks on April 18th. The water damaged thousands of homes leading to 75% of people being evacuated. The river finally crested on the 21st. The flood waters reached inland as far as 3 miles. The overall loss was over 2 billion.

Is it good to break flooding?

the flooding spread inland up to three miles from the riverbed.

The most amazing picture that remained etched in the memory of the nation was the blazing fire downtown surrounded by a sea of flood waters.

fresh water

Maslins took six weeks to return home.

Paul had helped out following 9 11.
He returned to Queens, his place of birth.

Some folks say 9/11.

2005 brought him south to Louisiana.
He had waited patiently for the call up.

It seemed different this time.
He always ran to help and be a savior.
This time around his effort resembled an act of escapism.

Did he have an existential issue with his life?

In his fifties his health had a few wrinkles. He had expressed a desire to slow down and promised this trip to be the last one for him.

CHAPTER 6

DAY ONE

EUGENE, OREGON

Joanne snapped out of her day dreaming. Questions loomed in her mind about the validity of her choice to embark on this journey. She wondered whether the hastiness of her decision would come back to haunt her. Was she cut out for this adventure? After all, the typical suburbia wife thrived on the mundane. She did not take risks, remaining safe in the comfort of her little nest she had taxingly built and the Ford expedition she drove.

Joanne worked as a part time psychiatric nurse at the Mercy Medical center next to the university. Her husband, a senior executive provided well for the family. She met him fifteen years ago when she was a young nursing student. He fell headlong in love with her and after a world wind courtship they married and she became a trophy wife. Soon they had three beautiful daughters. After the girls started school, Joanne returned to part time work just to get out of the house and not be so lonely when Tim her husband took those lengthy business trips.

The city of Eugene or the emerald city is nestled between the Cascade Mountains and the Oregon coast range, an area, well known for the Oregon wines.
This area, once the home of Kalapuya Indians, is replaced by upper middle class white households.
High heels replaced the moccasins.
Multi gabled houses with brick and stone facades and governor drives dotted the landscape once habituated by teepees.
It was indeed a beautiful country and the American way of life.

The Cuffs, the upper middle class family, lived in one of gated residential conclaves in the beautiful Willamette valley.
Joanne and her family took exotic vacations, travelling around the world.
They had three cars in their garages, and an in ground swimming pool with hot tub in the back.

They trekked to Spencer's butt along winding trails lined with lush green Douglas firs. They sailed on their 36 foot boat along the serene waters of the Fern Ridge Lake and they cycled through the endless paths along the banks of the Willamette River.

She had everything any American woman would want or did she?

Today Joanne Cuff was on her way to Mahlon Sweet Field. She had a flight to catch on the united express that would take her from the safety and sanctity of her all American family to the wilderness of the other America, on her way to cross the great cultural continental divide between the two Americas.

She wondered why?

Would it be the small receipt that she had noticed in her husband's slack pocket the other day?

CHAPTER 7

DAY ONE

MEMPHIS, TENNESSEE

Jill's NWA flight circled over the city that gave us the Graceland and Tennessee Williams. She had a layover of about two hours before connecting to Lafayette. She observed the pyramid that once housed the basketball teams in the skyline. It was as majestic as its ancient cousin in the name sake city in Egypt. Over the mighty Mississippi river she got a view of the three bridges spanning the river.

The sun shone and the outside temperature reached a pleasant 74 in contrast to the chilly fall in Pittsburgh. She looked at the over head monitors to locate her next flight. She was connecting on Mesaba airline from a corner of the C concourse. She stopped at the rest room to freshen up. At the mirror the dark rings under her eyes were staring at her. Those night mares were taking a toll.
She grabbed a coffee and sandwich and settled down to read. She had a hard time and did not get past the first page. He mind kept wandering, always returning to the lunch she had with Dr Higgins yesterday.

The lunch at Peter's pub in Oakland had the usual fanfare.

Jill always had her garden salad.
Walter often ordered a grilled Portabella sandwich. On a special day he would say "Oh I just have to run a couple of extra miles today."
He had ordered one of his favorite, a Philly steak sandwich without tomato or lettuce. He was a purist with Philly steaks.

Jill was off to Louisiana making this lunch a special occasion.

They had their differences but they agreed on the plight of the gulf coast.

Jill never understood her relationship with Dr.Higgin. A father figure, roles model a friend and a confidant but also someone she was attracted to. She always experienced a tinge of excitement round him.
Well, Walter, for his part, did not fathom their relationship either. Not sure what she was to him, he acknowledged their relationship to be complex with multiple striate of emotions including the envy he sensed when she got engaged.
He had watched with awe how she had changed in her social and political views.
He was proud of her and her trip.
He nodded in admiration...

"Call me daily ok. I want to live vicariously, the adventure you are plunging into Jill."

Jill promised she would and for the first time in their relationship he gave her an affectionate hug.

The music of Lara's theme from Dr Zhivago pulled her away from her day dreams, the ring tone of her cell phone

"Dr. Perkins?"
Jill heard a tentative female voice at the other end.

"Oh this is Joanne...." Followed by Silence.

"Dr Hesston gave me your number and said you are our team leader."

"My first team member!" Jill said to herself.

"I am Joanne Cuff. I will be flying out of Eugene, OR and will reach Lafayette in the evening. I am told to go to this B&B at Beaux Bridge. How do I get into that town?"
Jill felt totally lost and unsure for the first time. She would not recognize if Lafayette or Beaux Bridge hit her on her face.

"Joanne call me Jill and nice to meet you."

The ice broken, both of them anticipated the beginning of a wonderful fun filled friendship.

.

"Joanne, I maybe the leader, but I am as clueless as you are. I am at Memphis airport en route to Lafayette. The best option would be to catch a cab once you land .The cabbie certainly should know where to take you. I will see you in the evening”.

Jill already liked Joanne. She was looking forward to meeting her and working with her. She wondered how the other members of the team would be.

Jill realized that she could be using her cell phone a lot."I better check with Verizon wireless.”
She called the wireless company. When the operator came on, she identified herself.
“I am on a voluntary mission to LA and there is a good chance I will be using my cell phone a lot.”
To her pleasant surprise she was told that Verizon will write off any excess minutes. It was a token of appreciation.

Jill thanked the representative and went back to reading.

CHAPTER 8

DAY ONE

ACADIANA, LOUISIANA

Lafayette, the heart of Acadiana, has a population of about hundred thousand. Cajuns or those of Acadian decent formed the majority. The city, founded in 1821 by Jean Mouton, was Vermilion Ville after the river that ran through the town.
Six decades later, in honor Marquis de Lafayette, it settled on the present day name.

Acadiana with its 22 Louisiana parishes, stretching from just west of New Orleans to the Texas border, formed one of the colorful regions of the south.

This "Cajun country" compassing the southern and southwestern LA was unique in its culture.

Cajuns and Creoles along with others from Europe and Africa co inhabited the land. All the people of Acadiana were not Cajuns and all Cajuns were not direct descendants of folks of Arcadia.

The French speaking provincials lived in the maritime provinces of Canada; Nova Scotia, New Brunswick and Prince Edward Island. This region, especially Nova Scotia was designated as Acadia. The word Acadia, some say had its origins in Greek "Arcadia" an ancient Greek locale known for peace and rural tranquility. Others think it came from the Native American word "Akade" meaning paradise.

The explorer from Florence, Giovanni De Verrazanno, in 1524 called an area in outer bank as Acadia .This place is now known as Kitty Hawk North Carolina. Later the map maker Gastaleli delineated, Nova Scotia, further up the eastern Atlantic sea board as Acadia.

The first colony established in 1604 had the population mainly from the Centre Oust region of France. In the following times, they mixed, with others including the Irish, Scottish, English, and Basque, Spaniards and even Native Americans.

Through the years, until the treaty of Utrecht, when the French gave up the region to the British, this region remained under the control of the English and the French alternately. After the treaty, when the British became the rulers, decades of tension between the ruling Brits and the French Acadians citizens ensued, culminating in their expulsion in 1755 called the Le Grand De'rangement. Some of the expelled moved down to Louisiana. Unknown to them, the French had given Louisiana to the Spanish by that time.

The most famous poem of the area by HW Longfellow told the tragic story of Evangeline Bellefontaine traveling down the mighty river looking for her Gabriel Lajeunesse after being torn apart on their wedding day.

The Acadians, the sustenance farmers, further inter mixed with other settlers including the Germans, the French who came directly from France, the Spaniards, the later Anglo Americans as well as Native Americans and French creoles. This mixture of various ethnic groups formed a homogenous collection called Cajun permeated by the Acadian culture and they became the Cajun of today.

Ancelet et al: "Cajun country"; Brasseaux: "Acadian to Cajun" and "Founding of New Acadia", Dorman: "people called Cajuns" are three works that provides in depth details of the history.

The Cajun culture embodies the rustic provincial French. Shane Bernard in his book "The Cajuns-Americanization of a people" wrote that most Cajuns spoke French before WWII but in the last fifty years only a few can claim it to be their first language.

The Latin word "creare", meaning beget or create, forms the origin of the Creole. Later it became criollo in Spanish and then Creole in French, It might as well mean the people born in the new world but of those who came from France, Spain, Caribbean, Africa, Italy, also Indians and the Native Americans.

The Creoles are distinct from the Cajuns. They have differences in their culture, food, music, literature and have carried that down the centuries but there is also a certain wonderful union in all the aspects. One of the Cajuns once remarked that the main difference between the two was exemplified by their gumbo. The Cajuns don't like tomatoes in their gumbo.

In the Cajun country, the music is Cajun, Zydeco and the swamp.
The Cajun music had its roots in the French Ballads. They used the fiddle and the accordion.

Zydeco music had shades of African religious music.

And of course, there is the glorious Cajun and the Creole cuisines, food that is a gastronomic treasure and worth dying for.

The Cajun country has its rolling green hills in the north, the prairies in the middle, the bayous in the south and a marshy coastline. The main cities were Lafayette, Houma Thibodaux and Lake Charles. Lafayette is right in the heart….. the hub city.

The hurricanes Katrina and Rita, though, they did not strike physical harm to the city by their destructive fury, did cause significant psychological pain. By October 2005, the population of Lafayette had, according to most reports increased by 50%. This was population explosion caused by migrating victims of the hurricanes from two ends of the state.

Outside of the gulf coast area the victims were labeled as refugees.

In the last century the word refugee has been mainly reserved for people fleeing from one country to other (though by the narrow definition it could mean anyone leaving a calamity but usually never used that way) During the last hundred years, they were seen as poor, terrified, starving stigmata of mankind.

Those haunting images on the cover of many news magazines did more justice to someone aptly called alien than to the citizens of the super sized country. They were the icons of the third world countries and other violent conflicts.

When pictures of them in New Orleans, looking like those half naked urchins in some distant third world country, flashed all over the world ,it made many in America angry.

"How dare they show the God's own country, God's favorite country, in bad light to rest of the world?"

"They deserved God's wrath..."

They were the poor, the black and the ungainly underbelly of the richest nation on earth.
Some of the media labeled them scum, hooligans and behooved the horror on them. They were treated with the same distain as the degraded homeless, mentally ill and the starving poor in this country.

The bulk of them, who came from New Orleans and south east of the city like the Saint Bernard parish and Slidell, were creoles and Cajuns, The Rita victims were mainly the Cajuns.

As the unexpected visitors prolonged their stay in the fifth most conservative city in the country, the red carpet of welcome began to wear thin and tempers began to fly. This was evident in the articles of the local newspapers.

"There are more people, strangers hanging around the corner of Polk and Vermillion streets."
"The traffic is getting congested on Johnson Street and parking is getting to be a hassle."

In all fairness, the citizens of Acadiana were good hosts both to victims as well as the people who came to help. Some of them were extraordinary people.

Jim and Andrea Le Blanc; Mary and John Pellerin were all good citizens of Acadiana.
They were not just good they were exceptional human beings.

.

Jim and Andrea were married to each other. So were John and Mary.

To Jill they would become two of the best couples she has known in her life.

CHAPTER 9

DAY ONE

LAFAYETTE, LOUISIANA

Jill glanced out of the window of the plane. She searched for flooded land beneath.

"Don't be silly there is no flood in Lafayette" Jill said to herself.

"Funny how our mindset colors our perceptions." Jill had expected a raw visceral sense of calamity unfolding in front of her eyes.

Instead, she got the picture of a sleepy quaint town.

The Saab 340, a small jet prop plane, made an incipient landing and Jill discovered the magnitude of Lafayette airport. She did not find a taxi stand. A handful of people milled around.

She stood hundreds of miles away from home, in the hot southern gulf coast. She had come to help heal the emotional trauma. For the first time since the journey began, Jill was lost like a school girl.

She called John but got his Fax machine instead.
The only other person she knew would be Jim Le Blanc, the head of the regional the mental health system.

"Hello Mr. Le Blanc, this is Dr Perkins, I am deployed by SAMHSA to Lafayette for the next 2 weeks. You are my contact in Lafayette."

"Dr. Perkins we have been expecting you"

"I will send you our van to pick you up" Jill heard the soothing voice of Jim.

"Oh, by the way, there is a Dr. Hodge who is also waiting for a ride at the terminal. The two of you should meet and travel together."
Jill thanked Jim and went looking for Dr Hodge

Brian, after a tiring long flight, sat dozing on a bench. He had spoken to Jim not too long ago. This was his very first disaster deployment, and he was rearing to go and save souls.

"Excuse me"
"Are you Dr. Hodge by any chance?"

Brian woke up from his lazy slumber to find a beautiful woman.
"Yes I am"
"Good to meet you. I am Dr Perkins"
Jill stretched her hand in welcome.

"Jim told me you are waiting for the ride"

"You are the Dr Perkins?"

An uneasy sensation crept up Jill's spine.

"Yes I am the Dr Jill Perkins" asserted Jill.

"I had expected someone older and by the way, they just said Dr Perkins, I presumed you would be a man." Brian explained matter of fact.

Jill had mixed emotions about it all. Though flattered by the acknowledgement of youth and her sexuality, a nagging implication and tone of devaluation hung in the air.

She sensed some resentment in Brian's voice. He, an older white male, would be a subordinate of her. Little did they realize that this happened to be least of their contrasting views.

The uneventful ride, marred by a silence, spoke volumes to the uneasy truce between the two. The driver, a cheerful lady, tried her best to make them welcome to the city. Alas they were buried in their own thoughts.

The white agency van turned into the parking lot of the Mental Health center.

A middle aged bearded man greeted them at the main entrance. He introduced himself as the director for the region and their local contact, Mr. Jim Le Blanc.

Jim was a scaled down version of a teddy bear, someone who eluted warmth and caring. Jim appeared reserved. He spoke very few words and in soft low tones. But an aura of self assuredness and calmness surrounded him. He dominated the gathering just by his presence. His understated appearance was followed by the entrance of Andrea, another important leader of the regional mental health system.

She turned out to be the opposite of Jim in her personality, bountiful of energy, and chatted away as if Jill and Brian were her long lost pals.

They made the visitors comfortable and in earnest brought them up to speed. Andrea in her folksy way described the first days following the flooding. They had gone to New Orleans to help and were stranded on the overpass.
Jill remained quiet, taking it all in. She sensed the urgency in them and the momentous need for mental health in this area. Even these seasoned campaigners seemed affected by the hurricane.

Jill found them genuine, proud of their culture, gregarious in their southern hospitality and ready to work with the outsiders who had come offering a helping hand.

Jill and Brian decided to rent a car and share the ride. They met Angela,a nurse and a close friend of the Le Blanc's. She drove them to the Enterprise Rental on Johnson Street and they rented a cobalt.

Their journey took them through Lafayette city from Johnson Street to Ambassador Caffery parkway to Kaliste Saloom Road. They turned right into Green Tree drive and left on to east shamrock Road .They stopped when they came to a cul-de-sac.

Their dwelling for the next fortnight stood at the right, a half timber majestic Tudor home. A cute replica of the house that served as the mail box caught Jill's eye.

Their hostess Mary met them with warm inviting smile. She was a petite woman. Mary and her husband John turned out to be ~~a pair of~~ wonderful hosts.

John always tried to uplift their spirits with his folksy stories while Mary smothered all with attention and love.

Angela thought of introducing Jill and Brian to some real hometown Cajun cooking. They were naïve when it came to Cajun cuisine.

Jill found out the blackened red fish made famous by Chef Paul Delhumme may not Cajun after all. Tabasco hot sauce was not truly Arcadian in origin but was developed by McIhenny on the rural Iberian island of Avery. The Cajuns liked spicy food. It did not have to be nuclear. Cayenne pepper was added for the zing mostly.

Angela and Jill ordered a wonderful dinner of chicken and Andouille gumbo, catfish court bouillion and crayfish etouffee over rice and pecan pie for desert. Brian stuck with a juicy rib eye steak. His Cajun palate did not venture beyond McDonald's Cajun McChicken, beignet and chicory coffee.

When the gumbo arrived Brian stared at the goop. Jill noted the expression on his face and said "Brian did you not tell me that you are from Tuscan?"

"Yes I am"

"I have never been there, but isn't it a border town with melting of different cultures? I thought you would be exposed to various cuisines."

"Not me. I am a simple meat and potato guy""

"Spoken like a wasp."

Angela, a Cajun to core, took that opportunity to educate Brian.

"Brian, Gumbo, this muck, is a hearty soup that your mother would make."

"Not my mother" Bristled Brian.

"It has two parts, rice and the soup. Always the rice is added to the soup. The soup can be made of seafood, fowl, or other meat. The soup is thickened using Okra, file or Roux. The name Gumbo came from the central Bantu word Kigombo which meant okra."

When the crawfish etouffee arrived Brian almost had a fit seeing the little mudbugs on the plate.

Angela promised to introduce Brian to Boudin, Tasso, and Chitin in the near future.

On their return they found Paul sipping wine at the kitchen table and chatting with John. John had picked him up from the airport. After introductions, they settled down to chat.

Before long, Jill formed opinions about the two male members of her team. She thought Paul was an old pompous man and Brian a narrow minded bigot. Well she would come to know them in a different light during the coming days.

Joanne landed at the Lafayette airport later that evening; she did not find even one taxi waiting for fare. She began to panic. Then a cab, after dropping a passenger and on the way out, slowed down and Joanne flagged it down. The driver was in his twenties, dark complexioned, and spoke with an accent not familiar to her. She gave him the address of the B & B on John d Herbert Drive.

"Ma'am I am familiar with Breaux Bridge but I am not too sure about this location. It must be a new place... Would you rather stay in the city tonight, as it gets dark quickly, and look for the B & B in the morning? I know this little hotel where you could spend the night."

Joanne began to have misgiving about this taxi and its foreign sounding driver.
"No let's go to the B & B."

As the darkness fell and the town lit up, the cab took off on its way to Beaux Bridge.

From the terminal drive on to the SW Evangeline Throughway, they got on to the Interstate 10 East. They turned off at Beaux Bridge exit. Passing through the sleepy town the car headed towards the bayou.

The cabbie had been silent after the initial exchange. He played ~~this~~ strange music on his radio. It certainly was not English. She could make out the accordion and the fiddle as the main instruments.

In the stillness of the southern night, she felt lonely and alone for the first time. The excitement of this trip, to the unknown, was wearing off a little too quickly. She longed for the green hills of Eugene and the cool breeze of the northwest. Instead, stretches of water of the desolate swamps welcomed her.

“If he raped, killed and dumped me in the bayou no one would find out. I will be eaten by alligators”. Joanna said to herself getting apprehensive by the minute.

The thick opaque fog rendered the night starless. With poor visibility, it became harder to see what was in front of them and the dividing lines between the road and the swap turned murky.

“I should have just stayed home; I will never see my kids or my husband” sighed Joanne.

“Do you have any family?” Asked the driver.

"Why is he concerned? He is wondering if someone will look for me." Joanne wondered, and chooses to keep her counsel.

He suddenly pulled over.

“Here he comes” Joanne shivered in the hot southern night. He got out of the car and came over to her side.

“He is making his move.” She desperately looked for a weapon to protect herself.

He opened the door. She glimpsed his white teeth in the darkness and a rough hand stretching out to grab her. She sank back into the seat crouching away from her assailant.

Then he spoke.

“I think I recognize this place. I used to come to the here as a kid. The alligators will be out in the moonlight” he laughed.

“I want to show you the lake."
Joanne was not taking any risk. She visualized nothing but darkness,
She told the driver “Let’s find this place”

Past the lake sat the B & B. an old house that was recently renovated.
Glad to be in the safety of the owners, Joanne quickly went to the lighted entrance. She did give big tip to the cabbie for not killing her. He in turn thanked her.

He smiled and said “I thought you were taking me to some strange place. I could have been killed for the car and the money you know. I was so glad to come across the lake and realized I was familiar with this place.

He smiled again and drove off.
Joanne did not hold back tears of relief and laughed out hysterically.

When the owners started to talk, she realized that it was she who was the foreigner, speaking with a different accent.

Tammy landed in the dark. She wanted someone to pick her up. She phoned Jill, and the two men Paul and Brain went over to the airport to pick her up.

Neither of them thought to ask about her appearance when she called. At the airport they stood staring at very female who came out of the plane.
Then this dark haired girl wearing a tight fitting jeans and a denim shirt over a Tee came out and went to the car rental office. She had a good sized suitcase.

The two men inched their way towards the rental office. And Brian asked her.

"Are you from SAMHSA?"

"Oh yes I am Tammy, Tammy Peters."

"You must be the two boys that Jill sent for me" She said laughing,

"Should I rent a car?

"We don't know how many cars we would need. We can figure that out in the morning. We already have one car." Said Brian as they walked to the parking lot.

All the characters had finally landed.

CHAPTER 10

DAY TWO

Jill woke up in a strange bed and a stranger room. The bedroom walls were paneled with rich dark cherry in contrast to the pastel plaster of her home. A wonderful aroma floated in the air. It was the waif of cooking and baking. It flooded her memories with that of Mike who cooked breakfast on Saturday mornings. Her olfactory dendrites inhaled the scant of bacon, sausage and eggs.

She walked into the kitchen in her robe. John, busy taking, fresh baked bread out of the oven, lifted his head to greet her. She is the daughter I never had John said to himself admiring Jill with affection, She poured herself a cup of strong coffee. She always liked chicory in blend. Mary bustled about in the large dining room next door. She was chatting with Paul who was an early raiser.

The breakfast spread on the long and polished cherry table included fresh cut fruits, scrambled eggs, meats and good strong French coffee. Mary had place settings for each of them with fine china delicately placed over the French lace dollies. John and Mary had rolled out the red carpet for them.

This would be the morning ritual for the next two weeks to come.

Brian and Paul soon joined them at the table followed by Tammy.

“Good morning all. I can’t wait to start working with the poor victims” Brian sounded inpatient and noted that Jill was still in her robe.

“Hey, don’t we need to get to the center by 8 AM?”

Paul sensed the friction between the two and tried to lighten things up by saying.

“Surely they are not going to run away.” Everyone except Brian shared in the laughter.

“We have plenty of time; we meet up with the Le Blancs and will find out what they want us to do.”

"Dr. Hesston had clearly told me Brian, since we are the primary team here, things are fluid and we are at the disposal of the local mental health organization to use us as they seem fit which includes providing help to the stretched system, to the victims and to the first responders. We are not some fly by night rescue team."

Brian, stung by her rebuke, did not take the debate any further. The tension remained in the air and they finished their morning meal without further deliberations.

They trooped in to the car and drove to Dulles drive.

"I wonder why someone named a street after a Muslim" Brian asked rhetorically as they were driving along Kaliste Saloom Road.

"Why not? Maybe he did something important" Jill quipped

"Yeah right" Brian rolled his eyes.

Paul realized he and others will be subjected to some heated political and social debates in the days to come.

"We will meet Joanne; she is the last member of the team. I hope she got in alright. She was taking a cab to the other B & B" Jill informed the three.

They marched into Jim's office and from there they moved to the gym. This will be our daily meeting place. You can use the computers here." Jim offered.

The four of them dashed to the computer terminals, connecting themselves to their world, to check emails or Google. Jill leafed through her Medical Center exchange when someone called her name. She glanced up and noticed a striking woman standing over her.

"Dr Perkins you almost got me killed last night."
Jill, at loss for words, wondered what caused such a strong response in this stranger.
She noted Jill's discomfort, so she quickly added.
"I am Joanne"

She went on to tell them the story of her infamous cab ride and everyone including the uptight Brian appreciated the humor in the incident. Joanne had the quality to put people at ease.

Jim and Angela joined them. They brought in some boxes. SAMHSA had sent bright Orange tee shirts and back packs which were survival kits.

“Thank you for coming to Louisiana. We can use all the help and more.”
Jim started to talk, introducing him and Andrea to those who had not met them yesterday.
“We are short handed at the MHC. We need psychiatry presence at the main shelters; The Cajun dome, convention center and the shelter at New Iberia.”

“We have a special needs site at the Haymann center”
“They might ask for guidance at other places including the MHC at Crawley.” added Andrea.

Angela walked in.
“We need to checkout a shelter in Cypremort point. There is no response from them."

“Why don’t we all go, that way our guests can get a grasp of the disaster?” Andrea responded.

They packed into the white van and left for Cypremort point. They had a hard time locating the turn off point of Route 90 because the winds of Rita had blown the signs away. They wandered along the circular state road 83 lined by sugarcane fields. There, they started to experience the furry of Rita .A "million elephants" had stampeded through them. They spied a huge barge sitting on land. Nature’s hands had violently plucked it from the inter coastal water way and placed it on dry land.

Finally, after many trials, they made it past Louisa and reached Cypremort. The road narrowed and along the way to Cypremort point, miles of destroyed houses and camps, the vacation or weekend abodes, greeted them. The few fortunate structures left standing had brown demarcating lines along the walls at 15 feet above ground, the calling card left behind by the rushing flood surge.

The trip finally ended at Cypremort Point. The reclusive Point jutted on to the watery expanse of the Vermilion and Weeks bays on one side and West Cote Blanche bay on the other.

The scene had changed dramatically.

They stood solemnly at the edge of the water, all seven of them, looking towards Marsh Island with its wild life refuge; the shell keys and the wide calm blue of Gulf of Mexico beyond.

Not a word was uttered. There was no need to say anything at all.

Even Andrea, who always had something funny to say, remained subdued. Brian refined from his customary wise crack.

They stood in awe.

The blue serene waters, without a single wave breaking at the rocky shore line, spoke volumes of nature's omnipotence.

The total silence sent a shiver down Jill's spine. Paul's soothing hand on her shoulder comforted her.
The instant their eyes met, they knew what the other was going through. Paul gently squeezed her shoulder and Jill moved closer towards Paul.

Paul had been there. He had experienced the pain of helplessness. Though he did not know her story, he noted similar emotions in Jill's eyes.

Tammy, Joanne and Brain all appreciated the poignant moment.

They were looking at the power of nature magnified through its absolute calmness.

It seemed like ages but Andrea finally broke the spell and brought them back to reality.

"Let's go look for the shelter"

They searched for the building in vain. They did not find any in the sea of devastation. The desolateness was engulfing.

They came upon a church.

The holy floor was covered in a foot of dirt, with nothing left to salvage.
The house of God was demolished. Nature did not spare even the hallowed ground.

As they were leaving, with some disenchantment, Jill came upon, in this total disarray, three, foot high figurines arranged in a corner.
It was the holy family.
The statures sat quietly in the corner undisturbed.
Interestingly they noted one little thing. There weren't any foot prints leading to or away from the grotto.

They continued their journey to inter coastal city, on the Vermilion Bay. They found shrimp boats and larger trawlers sitting on land. A few of them upright, others on their sides, and one was even upside down. Covered with mud, they sat there like ghosts of a pantomime.

They went by a cemetery. The above ground graves churned up by the hurricane, lay splattered all over. Even in death, humanity, was not spared the furry.

They visited the school at Erath
Jill picked up pictures and drawing by children and wondered were those kids were now. A somber flash back of floating bodies startled her reality.

On their return to the base, they continued to drive through miles of wind and surge damage. The outward trip had intermittent gasps of disbelief but now emptiness and a cloud of depression surrounded them. The enthusiasm of these altruists had evaporated.

Their field endeavor had turned sour. The devastating snapshots of Rita, only a few miles from the tranquility of the quaint towns like Lafayette Crawley and Beaux Bridge became stark reminders of the job ahead.

Back in the city, after a quick lunch at the local Creole restaurant, where most of them ate fried cat fish and dressing, they returned to the center.

From the Center they sped through Dulles on to Bertrand and then turned into west congress and finally reached the Cajun dome which was the home of the Ragin Cajuns and Lady Cajun basket ball teams.

The Dome still housed thousands of evacuees. At the height of occupation, they held several thousands more. Reminiscent of the superdome and the conventional center in New Orleans albeit the horror stories associated with it, it had a hallo of forbiddance in spite of hoards of law enforcement officers of all shades, city officers, state troopers and National Guard.

They walked towards the imposing dome, through the near empty parking lots. The official vehicles, military humvees, police cruisers, fire trucks and ambulances surrounding a bank of satellite antennae were the only ones parked there. It was a far cry from the days of the Saturday football games of the Ragin Cajuns.

"Ah, this reminds me of the pictures on the TV?" Tammy remarked softly.

Everyone knew the significance of her statement, and heads nodded in silence.

Check points with metal detectors guarded the entrance. The national guardsmen in full battle regalia greeted them as they passed through these portals. The war weary guardsmen and women with their M16 dangling from their shoulders were the sentinels.

They had returned from Iraq to another set of horrors.

The young guardsman checked the face with the SAMHSA ID.
"Mental health yeah?"
"We need a lot of that around here starting with Me." he spoke to nobody in particular, in his flimsy effort at humor and a thin veil over his anxiety and fatigue.

The controlled environment pleasantly surprised them but as they turned the corner, they ran headlong into a flood of milling population.

Jill experienced a slight uneasy sensation, a bit nauseous and queasy in her stomach.
"It's just a little anxiety girl." she said to herself. “What else did you expect?”

As she moved forward, carried in part by the motion of the human movement, she quickened her pace. She headed further through the double doors.

And then, she stood at the threshold of the dome.

The vastness of the cavernous dome stretched in front of her, but all she perceived was rows and rows of beds draped in green sheets.

A stream of sweat flew down the side of her face along her sharp cheek, the ankle of the jaw and on to her blouse. Her heart pounded and she heard and sensed the palpitations against the rib cage.
Her hands shook and finding it hard to breath, she was light headed and dizzy.
She gasped for air, hungry to fill her oxygen starved lungs with air. Her one hand clutched her side while the other was over the left breast.

“Oh my God what’s happening to me?”
“I am having a heart attack”
Jill felt excruciating pain over the sternum and the left of her breast bone.

“I am dying”

Her feet lost its sensation and the feel for the ground beneath her.

This dreaded episode reached a crescendo.
Her eyes glazed over with sweat and tears.

"I have to escape"

“I have to get away to safety or I would die here” Just like Mike in the subway.

She ran back through the double doors and past the escalator and through the side doors and into fresh air and blue skies, into an alleyway between the dome and the convention center.

She filled her lungs with oxygen.
Her relief from impending doom was short lived.
She was back among the crowd.
The walls of the building began to close around her and sweaty bodies pressed against her.
She lost touch with reality.
She envisaged her body a few feet away and she glimpsed Mike in a white robe waving and beckoning her.

The sound of the subway....
Explosion of the IED s like fireworks on Fourth of July....
Rattle of gun fire as bullets shatter Mikes head.....

There were checkered turbans everywhere and the English accent was drowning out the rappers in the background.

"Die you white pig." blared the turbaned. Not in Arabic or Harlem English but in clipped British.

She crouched in a corner doubled up and vulnerable.
Waiting to die!

That's how Paul found Jill.

He had been worried. She had been away only for a few minutes. From what he had learned about her in the last two days it was so unlike her. Paul had gone looking.
He sat next to her wrapping his arms around her and holding her close to him. He heard her sob.
He let the closeness of their bodies and beating of their hearts sooth her.

"OH my, Paul where are we? "Jill regained her composure.
"Jill you are ok. I think you felt faint and had to sit down. It must be all the heat." Paul commented.

She did not challenge his explanation though she was quite certain of Paul's lie.
"Shall we find the others?"
"Sure Paul"

Jill got up, tossed her hair and reverted right back to looking formal and professional.
Without much adieu they, went in search of the other three stragglers.

A few feet down the path, Jill broke silence.
"And Paul, not a word of this to others!"

Paul just nodded
They met up with the Red Cross brass. They soon realized the regimental rigidity of this organization.

The Red Cross ran a monolithic behemoth ship with little leeway for the abstractness of human emotionality.
Jill rose to the challenge. Walter always praised her for her diplomacy when it suited her agenda.

She said "We are placing ourselves under the Red Cross command."

That was an ice breaker.
Now all they needed to do would-be to educate the bureaucrat, the distinct difference between law & order and mental health.

"Jill that was capitulation" Brian complained later.

"Not at all my friend, on the contraire, this way, we keep a low profile and do what we came here to do without stepping on toes" she retorted.

Paul did not hide his amazement how wise their youthful leader was, certainly not the cowering little girl he had seen not too long ago.

"Dr Perkins, you can give any one a run for their money"

Subtly she was also establishing the hierarchy. She had to put Brian in his place. There was only one leader and that was her. She did not want the next two weeks to be a long drawn tug of war between her and this snooty sexist. Once

hatched down, they brooded on their own and that suited them quite well.

They met members of another group, the Volunteers of America,
Some of them, evacuees themselves, did wonderful work with the population. They became close allies in identifying people in need.

Tammy roamed along the rows of beds in the dome.

Suddenly she stopped short in her tracks.

At first, she did not recognize what she had walked into.

She froze. Her legs would not carry her any further. She found herself on the stage of an unfolding tantalizing drama.

She stepped back between the row of green beds, and from the shadows she watched in disbelief, as she realized that a couple in the adjacent bed was making love.

What the....
Tammy blushed at first but that turned in to embarrassment when the woman, in her forties, who was riding the man stopped in mid stream, looked up, and her eyes locked with those of Tammy.

The eyes showed mixture of passion and amusement but not an iota of shame.

Tammy agonized over the nakedness of her clothes than the nudity of the woman who said.
“It has comes down to this. We have lost everything including any thread of civility.”

“This 8x6 area holds everything we have.”
“We do not have any privacy.”
“We have turned to carnal exercises, to keep our sanity and dignity, though we are fucking like animals.”
Her pretty tanned face burst into peals laughter breaking through the dark cloud of anguish.

“Don’t stop now Hun” the woman’s husband said as he grew excited.

Through the excited moaning of the man, she gleefully exhorted the man.
“Oh yeah baby. Take me like you had me in the attic, while we waited to be rescued”

She restarted her rhythmic banging.... her lustful hip crashing again his pelvis.
"Ride cow girl ride." encouraged the man in their quasi obliviousness to the presence of Tammy and the rest of universe.

In this sexual vacuum, their excitement flourished.

"Oh baby"

"Faster Hun"

"Fuck harder"

"Harder"

As she moved up and down on him, riding him like a bronco, his erection slid in and out of her wetness.

Tammy stood mesmerized. She watched with her eyes wide open shut.

Then they climaxed.

They came together with a million exploding stars, just like their first time decades ago.

Without a word they lay in each other's arms, in love.

Tammy silently exited, kicking herself for intruding into their world or what was left of it.

A world defined geometrically by 48 square feet.

All of 8 feet by 6 feet!

Joanne came across her first patient.
A big man with beady eyes, visibly agitated, Joanne knew the look. She had seen one too many of those in the detox wards back home.

Sweating,
Dilated pupils, tearing, yawning,
Runny nose, the runs, abdominal cramps.

He had it all like a text book case.

He grabbed her badge and yelled.
“Mental health!”

He demanded that she give him something for his heroin withdrawal.

"Oxycontin?"
"Vicodin?"
"Seroquel?"

"Not even vistoril?"

“No not even methadone” Joanne said walking away.

Joanne realized that they had no medications for their patients.
She went looking for her friends. She made a mental note to talk to Jill, Dr Perkins, about disaster pharmacotherapy.

She soon found even the utterance of the magic words of lethality did not guarantee a bed in the hospital and the medication formulary stayed skeletal at best in the cash strapped state.

Jim and Andrea shared their thoughts on their guests
“I think they are good people” Andrea mused.
“I agree they are dedicated, competent and willing to help."
"Oh and by the way, the state of LA has approved Dr Perkins temporary medical License. That must be the fastest ever…. less than 24 hrs!"
"And she has privileges at the hospital too.”

“They were pretty shook up with what they experienced out there today informed Andrea. She had wondered if she had exposed them a little too much too quick.

They were soon joined by the famous five. Jim opened the discussion on what was on tap for the next two weeks.

“The staffing here at the center was ok pre hurricanes but now we are stretched “Jim showed first signs of faint stress.

“We need some doc time Dr Perkins”
Jill agreed to function as a psych ER/evaluation/follow up doc at least part time.
"Paul can do the inpatient work."

“We need a body at Crawley, another center east of here. They are swamped even worse than us.”
Joanne volunteered herself to be the one to head east.

“Joanne, your job also includes helping to tie up the loose ends at the New Iberia shelter. You are the ideal person since you live in Beaux Bridge." Andrea added.

“The other two can comb the dome.”

“Jill will cover their medication needs.”

That encapsulated the work schedule for the coming days.

The shadows of the night had cast their long arms by the time they finished.

It had been a hard day.

They knew they would be working long hours .They had expected primitive work settings. Instead, they expressed their gratitude for clean sheets and great food.

Back home at shamrock, Mary the resident historian, enlightened them with the story behind Kaliste Saloom road, named after a famous native of Lafayette, Judge Kaliste Saloom. He was a special agent in the counter intelligence corps in Europe and Africa during WWII. After the war, he returned home and started his law firm. He went on to serve as a judge.
Yes, they were descendant from people from eastern part of the world, Lebanese and Christians.

Jill coyly smiled at Brian.

Mary had put together a light supper.
Sadly, the sights and happenings of the day had drained their appetite.

Joanne took Jill aside during supper to ask her if she could move in with them.

"It's a great idea. Let me talk to the hosting committee. Also you have work at New Iberia for a couple of days"

They had traveled together, just the two of them, because Joanne had to stop and rent a car. Jill drove back to the enterprise store on Johnson Street. In the morning the inn owner had given her a ride into town. On return, Jill realized that Joanne is turning into a significant person in her disorganized life.

Jill talked to Mary and they planned to shift Joanne to Mary's house so that all of them will be at the same place. Joanne would move to a room next to Jill's.

Jill Munched on a Pooboy as she checked off the last few things she had to do.

Talk to Dr: Hesston; a daily thing to do.

Call Dona and ask her to contact every drug detail person in Pittsburgh to have them Fed Ex samples to her at Lafayette.

Calling Dr. Higgins was the last item on the agenda. They talked and Jill blurted out the story of her panic attack followed by the flash back.

Walter down played the story and there was the reinforcement of the subconscious conspiracy between the two.

Sitting down she reflected on the day for a short while and then hit the sack.

CHAPTER 11

DAY THREE

Another day in Lafayette.

Jill and the crew returned to the Center.

The Center is like any other mental health place around the country.

Decades ago,
The society, led by bleeding heart liberals, decided that the mental asylums, also known fashionably as state hospitals, had the label of "too inhuman for the 20th century America."

It is true that many lost souls had been languishing in the backwards of these hospitals and their conditions were of Papillion proportions.

Morally challenged by movies like “one flew over the cuckoo’s nest”, they opened the flood gates of these institutions to herd them out into the wide open spaces of the society.

It was a rude awakening for both.

The residents had long lost the ability to lead an independent existence and the society realized that these mentally ill are misfits in the white picket fence neighborhoods.

"Free at last but not in my back yard" seems to be the mantra across the nation.

The care of these victims of mal adaption fell on the sagging shoulders of the community mental health centers. They were further demolished and demoralized by the indifference of the self-indulgent Reagan era.

The mental health center in Lafayette had a vibrant outpatient unit. It also has a small inpatient unit run by the university.
Jim introduced Dr Perkins to the outpatient staff, glad to utilize the services of Jill even if it was for just a few days. The deluge of patients flowing from either direction took a toll on the doctors here at the clinic.

"A professor from north has come down to help us out." he told the staff. Though the youth and the gender of this professor had detractors among the staff, they were all happy to receive any help they could get.

Louisiana mental health system cried out for help even before the hurricanes.
No wonder Jill got her license in record time.

Many mentally ill human beings needed care and Jill's attention.

On her way she ran into some short coats. This is the acronym for medical students. They are the enthusiastic "colts" jockeying for attention. They are greenhorns trying to sort out their role in the medical world. They were six medical students from NO. As the city went under so did their medical school program. The students, left without a hospital, professors or patients, migrated to Lafayette. Their quest for salvaging the current academic year landed them at the center and they were flying aimlessly like sea gulls in Pittsburgh till they met Dr Perkins.

Jill felt sorry for them and she took them under her wing. "You can follow me." I am a professor in Pittsburgh.

"Clinical bedside teaching is what I do in my real job at Pitt Medical School, so I would love to teach you guys at least for the next few days."

These students, an enthusiastic bunch, had been at the beginning of their third year, the year they become real doctors. It was the crossing of the threshold, when they get to wear the white coats, hang the stethoscope around the neck and wander the hospital hallways following the clinical parade.

The teaching hospital clinical parade is always choreographed.
The attending doctor is the fearless leader at the vanguard the minions adoringly followed.
There is always a MC. That role was filled by a fellow or a chief resident. Dr. Perkins had been in both those shoes before her ascension to her citadel. The MC would walk

half a step behind the boss. This junior leader or the XO as navy might call them, always had the attending's ear while he or she orchestrated the band behind them.
The entourage would be a heterogeneous collection of junior residents, interns and the lowly medical students bring up the rear. At the big house, this collection included other students like the pharmacy and nursing students.
The only time these minnows got any attention was when the attending threw them a curve ball, a question that the residents and the interns very skillfully managed to avoid while keeping a face of smug know it all.

This pack of six yearned for knowledge. And they were close to the teacher without any fellows, residents or interns to keep them away from the attending.

Concurrently they all had deepening furrows of financial burden. The higher education system at the ivory towers of learning continued to come with its "plastic "baggage.
They had graduated from the undergraduate college with drowning loans. The four years at the medical school poured more dirt into the tomb of financial slavery.
Each day they were sinking deeper into debt but they had nothing to show for their misery.

"We are born free but only a few live free."Most of us are doomed to the economic slavery symbolized by the shinning plastic". Jill concluded.

"There is a suicidal patient who needs to be evaluated Dr Perkins. He might have to be hospitalized."

“Ok guys; let’s walk over to the holding room and interview him.”

The six whispered among themselves “wow our very first suicidal patient.”

“Not really, my roommate was suicidal.” One of them giggled as she fondly remembered the day she and a few of her friends got intoxicated.
They could hear voices as they rounded the corner. Two male voices and they appeared to be in a heated discussion.

“Wait, let's listen to them. You can learn a lot about a person’s psychological condition just by listening” Jill’s out stretched hand brought the convoy to a halt.

Jill gestured them to silence so that they could hear the patient. She wanted them to learn the various aspects of history taking, the verbal and the non verbal cues.

It looked like they were catching the latter half of a debate about music and musicians and maybe a lot more.

“I liked them as singers, they are sexy and have amazing voices, but they have no place in politics. They should just shut up and sing.”

“Who says so? They have equal rights, like you and I, to nail the elected officials asses to the truth and assail them about the way they are running the country.”

“But they were insulting our president in time of war for crying out loud. We do not want anyone giving aid and comfort to our enemies. It is like they were insulting the country and the flag and bashing us all.”

“We Americans are not only fickle and egocentric but we blindly spout psycho typically juvenile exceptionalism. Our nation has a populace in preformal stage of development. They can see only white and black and are blind to the vastness of grey. Their minds are so small they cannot appreciate the difference between the country and its government.”

“The true patriot stands up and points out the wrong doings of the public servants including the president. He is not King George you know.”

“It took the little boy to shout, the emperor wore no clothes while the rest of the empire maintained polite silence.”

“Let the one who have not sinned cast the first stone”

“Thrashing is for idiots and bigots and those who don’t like the beignets.”

Those soufflés and roulettes would spread love all over the world.”

“Yes he might be the C in C but George is not my god.”

“Who are you anyway?”

I am Leonardo, the one and only Da Vinci”

There was long hysterical laughter followed by deep sobbing.

Until that time even Jill had a hard time differentiating between the guard and the guarded.

She moved into their view.

There were two men in the small room the size of a 10 x 10 bedroom except there was no furniture.

A tall burly young man sat on a chair wearing a uniform that declared him to be the guardian angel. He stood up and sheepishly said.

“Hello doctor, we were just chatting.”

He realized that the banter had got a bit too personal.

He let them all pass, though the students choose to hide behind the safety of the security officer.

This was their tryst with the “Da Vinci”

He huddled in a corner. He stood up as Jill approached him and she could hear a collective breath of apprehension from behind her. Dr Perkins, always aware of her surroundings and the potential threat from her patients did not sense any animosity radiating from this soul.

He stood tall, easily six foot and more but slender with Romanesque features. He had long blond hair which hung in unruly locks with a matching beard. His eyes were as blue as Jill's. Dressed in a long shapeless cloak and leather sandals he had an uncanny resemblance to Jeffery Archer.

There was our messiah.

The only thing that was not picture perfect notably was a long aquamarine plume of feather that gloriously spread skyward from a dark baggy hat.

He appeared to be an amalgam of Jesus Christ and Leonardo Da Vinci except for the plume.

"I am Dr Perkins."

"Hey Doc, JC here, are you going to crucify me? Or lock me up and throw the key away?"
Again there was rapture of laughter and the plume swayed back and forth mesmerizing the students. Through the shadows of the plume streams of tears flowed down his sharply chiseled cheeks.

"Is he crying or laughing?" whispered one student to other.
"I think both." said a third.

When he realized their focus of attraction, he bellowed, "That's my voodoo outfit.
I am not JC I just play one."
"I know, Jesus, like me was bisexual. How else would you explain his love for Mary Magdalene and John the apostle?"
"Have you seen the last supper fresco on the walls of Santa Maria Della Grazie in Milan?"

“Wow; Cecilia, Lucerzia, and Lisa all together.” said JC in awe looking past Jill and staring at three bewildered female medical students.

‘My, my, this must be my lucky day I have never had the attention from so many pretty women.” He reverted to being human again and flirtatious.

“But that are not our names.” came the meek protest.

Jill, will a smile on her face pointed out. “He is talking about Cecilia Gallerani, Lucerzia Crivelli and of course Lisa Del Giocondo better known as Mona Lisa, the three renaissance women of Da Vinci.”

Turning to Jill he ventured. “You Dr Perkins are Beatrice d’Este.”

“I am flattered but I don’t look anything like the Duchess of Milan.”

“Ah, a shrink with a love of art”

Jill is not a connoisseur of art. She and Mike, who loved art, had travelled extensively through western Europe and some of it had rubbed off on her from seemingly endless boring hours at the Louvre, Uffizi, Academia and Musei Vaticani to name a few.

“JC why don’t you come with us to some where we can sit and chat?”

“Officer we are going to take JC into our office if that’s ok with you”

"Don't give the Doc a hard time man." said the guard. He was relieved to be off guarding the suicidal maniac. Now he could go and have his cigarette.

Jill marched the whole entourage to the office.
After seating everyone, she started her psychiatric interview.

"You always start with an open ended question." She told the students.

"So JC. What is happening?"

"Not too good doc."

"Do you mind tell us your story, these students would benefit?" Jill asked pointing to the eager beavers.

"Sure doc, anything for a pretty doc." He flirted with Jill again.

Even Susan the "Lisa Del Gioconda" couldn't help laugh at his gregarious attitude.
They all noted how pressured his speech was and how his mind danced over a thousand colors of ideas.

"I am thirty years old and I have been a bipolar for about 10 years, the first 5 being undiagnosed. "

"Why don't you tell us your story and not your diagnosis?" directed Dr Perkins.

“I was a freshman at the university of Norte Dame,” he laughed.

“Don’t you get the irony of my schism?” staring from face to face disappointed that even Jill the “art lover” did not get it.

“My majors were Mathematics and art and I did a minor in music. I planned to be the next Leonardo Da Vinci, the architect, painter, inventor extraordinaire.” he winked.

“Da Vinci, the ultimate renaissance man studying at Norte Dame the symbol of Gothic art, “explaining disparagingly to the novices.

“Of course, you are talking about the Cathedral of Norte Dame,” the gothic masterpiece on Ile de la cite on the river Seine in the heart of Paris. Even Jill had a hard time keeping up with the flight of ideas and JC’s juxtapositions.

Towards the flag end of the freshman year, his friends and professors began to notice a transformation in the reticent kid.

“Hey slow down man, you are like the energizer bunny.” they used to caution me.

He got involved in one too many activities. He just had to do one more and he had all the energy for it. His roommate could not sleep as he kept him up most of the night. He indulged feverishly in one project or the other. He felt the world moved too slowly for his taste. The walls of the room were covered with miles of paper. Some of them showed evidence of his affection for renaissance painting and, Romanesque architectural drawings.

He also had a lot of nonsensical writings and drawing.

He had his favorite Da Vinci cap on his table .One night some prankster placed a tin foil hat right next to it.

In the class rooms he because erratic and irritable. He challenged the professors with his grandiose plans and theories. His speech remained pressured and he could not be disrupted in his endless monologues.

The project he had with three others came to an impasse because he indulged in irrelevancy.

He started experimenting with recreational pharmacopoeia. Speed was his drug of choice and he washed them down with gallons of the Irish brew.

The transformation of the ex altar boy became complete when he began his journey through girlfriend experience of the full service escort services at $100 per hour.

"Oh, when I was young, this old priest molested me. Should I tell you that in detail?"

"Sure why not, if that is important to you, but shall we reserve it for later?"
Dr. Perkins sensed the initial cringe followed by the sigh of relief from her apprentices'.

She wanted to keep the distractions to minimum and get to the bottom line. Was this man suicidal and if so, how she would she get him in the most realistic and appropriate treatment setting.

"I felt I was wasting my time in the United States. So I flew to Italy, to the land of Leonardo.

"I came to Florence, the city of renaissance, in the heart of Tuscany."

I saw the David at the Academia and went up the tower in the Dumo.

"I waited in line to visit the Uffizi galleries. As the line wound around the courtyard it was close to the river. I could see the Ponte Vecchio Bridge over the Arno River. Then something came over me."

"Hours later I woke up in an Italian hospital. In a straight jacket and they had shot me up with a lot of haldol. "

"They told me that I had dived in to the river from the parapet proclaiming that I could fly."

"Weeks later I flew back to New York. No one at state side knew where I was.
The story flew out at a torrential rate and the students had a hard time keeping up.

"Since then I have tried to kill myself many times. Mainly when I am down."
'I had many hospitalizations spread across five states. I have been on every imaginable psych medications and I even had ECT."

"The last time I was in the hospital, three years ago, they gave me ECT. After a course of 22 ECT I came out of the deep depression. Lithium, Depakote and Trileptal. Combination appears to hold me in a stable state."

“Then I came to New Orleans.”

JC aka John Connor was an expat from New York, a musician of some repute and had transplanted himself from the big apple to the big easy.

He played his sax along Rue Royale in the French quarters when in sanguine mood. He, in less extravagant times, waited tables at the court of two sisters during the day and did a jig at one of the many dancing bars along Bourbon Street.
For the last three years he had been a NO musician and bipolar resident.

“You worked at the two sisters?” asked Jill incredulously.

“I love that place. The best place to eat. Oh their Jazz brunch is worth dying for.” She added.

If London was their favorite European playground NOLA was the erotic stomping arena.

Mike and Jill would jet son to NO on many a Friday evenings to spend the week end in the erotic decadence.

Court of the two sisters historically started as a high end fashion shop. The Creole sisters Emma and Bertha Camors started their notions shop where the rich ladies were entertained. Over years it became a restaurant and passed through many owners. It had been a landmark in the French quarters at 613 Royal Street.

The romantic courtyard with the wisteria vines took her back to the majestic times when the French Creole ruled New Orleans...
"One can sip a mint Julep, listen to the jazz trio and be transported back into that time."

Fabulous food included shrimp Creole omelets and boiled crawfish with remoulade.

There are heaps of ceviche and pâtés.

Duck a la orange, veal grillades and gravy, ettufe é, and prime rib with horse radish are few of the entrees.

Banana foster, topped with vanilla ice cream and praline sauce; Bread pudding with whiskey sauce and Mardi gras king cake lead the desert spread.

All this is drowned in carafes of Mimosa, an orange and champagne cocktail.

Jill had drifted in to a dissociative state before he brought her back. She noticed that that dissociation had become too easy for her these days.

"Doc, I have been without medications for the last few weeks. When Katrina came by I lost my doc, clinic and medications."" Who Knows? Maybe my Doc at the memorial hospital clinic drowned!"

"I have been feeling strange this time. I feel both happiness and sadness at the same time."

"Let me ask you JC, are you feeling that you want to hurt yourself?"

“Honestly Doc, I don't. But that is between the two of us. This is the only way I can get any medical attention.”

Jill knew the power of the magic word so well. She despised the system that forced sick people to lie. The psychiatric patients frequently uttered the magic word of suicide to get into a hospital.
In Louisiana the magic word was a must to get you into the outpatient system leave alone an inpatient set up.

“JC let me lay it out to you. I am going to say you cannot guarantee safety outside the hospital. I want to get you hospitalized; get you back on your medications and hopefully back on the streets.”

“Thanks and spoken like a Duchess.” JC laughed out.

After she took him back to the safety officer, they were back in the office.

Turning to the students Jill said “He is bipolar and is in a mixed state during this episode. That’s why he has coexisting opposite emotions.”

She was ready for the bureaucratic hassle. She called the university hospital.
She got the resident on call.

“I have this pt with me and I need to hospitalize him because he is suicidal.”

“I am sure he is.” The resident replied sarcastically. It was no secret that the university ER did not enjoy babysitting a suicidal patient in their 23 hr slot until a bed opened up.

“I am going to send him over.”
“Do I have a choice?”

“No you don’t.” laughed Jill.

“And while you have him I want you to put him back on his medications. Start him on 1000mg bid of Depakote, 300mg bid of lithium and 150mg bid of Trileptal.”
She had no qualms about loading him up.
That was the end of the exchange for the day.

The pt would sit in the observation bed for 23 hrs. If lucky, he would be admitted, if not, he would be back again, to be part of this façade and merry go round.

“At least they would start him on his lithium, Depakote and Trileptal." Jill told the students.

She knew that more than likely, they would run into JC again.

Tammy and Brian were making rounds at the Dome.
Less than couple of minutes into their morning, they ran into Tanya.

Tanya was an Afro American girl in her twenties. She had just returned from a meeting with the FEMA official and she was not a happy camper.

The weasel from the federal government, a heartless automaton in a white planter's hat, had told her that she and many others like her from her neighborhood would never be returning to their homes.

She remained almost certain that she had seen a shimmer of gloating, a gleam of unabridged gratification for the ethnic cleansing in his beady eyes.

An air of apprehension transuded through the Dome. What would happen to her house and her ancestral land, the hallowed dirt that belonged to her family for four generations? Is this going to be the next great migration northwards?

She sat on bed with her 5 year old girl on her lap. Tammy could sense her despair as they walked up to her.

"We are from SAMHSA .Can we help you?" asked Tammy in her customary non threatening charming southern voice.

"NO" Tanya said curtly and turned away from the two white folks.

"You look sad." patronized Brian.
Something in Brian's tone set Tanya off.

They were quite unprepared for the barrage of rancorous monologue that hit them next.

"Why don't you take your pseudo philanthropy and shove it?"

"You white people are pretentious and ostentatiously arrogant."

"You come here with your condescending and disdainful empathy, thinly veiled in your altruistic and munificent façade that has evolved into a travesty, a charade of handouts and sham sympathy."

"You are all the same, another embellishment on the embroidery in the intrinsically racist tapestry of modern day American feudalism, just like the president, the governor, Oreo mayor, the homeland security and the FEMA."

"We don't want your charity or pity. We can make it on our own, just leave us alone."

"Where was the national Guard when my Grandma was dying of thirst?

"Where were the boats when my mother got swept away in the torrential waters?"

"You should have waited for a few more days; we would be dead statistics too."
"That would have been four less to worry about."

Brian was stunned. The savior's cloak was not so shinning white anymore. It became splattered with the colored vitriolic.
Before, he could open his mouth in defense of his race, his profession, and above all his very own self against this fragile young Afro American woman, she continued.

"You folks think of us as less than human"

“But then, why blame you personally; your fathers treated us as property, to be traded like some baseball cards with impunity.”

“When we tried to scavenge food and water for our little ones you shot at us like dogs.”

Brian turned red, a clear sign of the raising frustration, incredulity and anger. They had come to help these people and this woman chastised them without an iota of gratitude. "You could have left when you were told to!"“He finally interjected.

“You sanctimonious bastard” she stared at Brian with blazing eyes.

“What would you know?”
“You are the embodiment of the self righteous ersatz American multitude.”

His usual demeanor was crumbling.
Never before had anyone so blatantly massacred his assiduously fashioned persona.

He turned and walked way.

Tammy had to run to catch up with him. She grabbed his arm.

“We cannot just walk away like that Brian."

“Sure I can. Did you not hear all the hatred she was spewing against us? What an unappreciative lot.”

“She is one of those welfare mothers, turning out babies like rabbits.”

“She is one of those parasites living off the hard earned money of us taxpaying white folks.”

Now it was Tammy’s turn to be angry. She had been bombarded with similar opinionated utterances in the last few years.

“Brian, enough, you know better than that. We should go back to her”
She was already on her way back and Brian had no choice but to follow.

They quickly realized that this woman had heard Brian’s comments.

“For centuries your people enslaved, exploited and lived off the blood and sweat of my people. I don’t want your help. I can take care of myself.”
“Unlike your many poisonous myths, there are more white welfare mothers than black.”
"I am going to graduate school for my MSW. I have two degrees in English literature and history.”

“We owned the house like the 60% in the lower 9th ward. Though poorer than the bohemian French quarter, we had honest jobs. We were not all drug dealers, gangsters or low life like they made us out to be”.

The grand finale of her oratory fireworks followed.

Something that even Tammy had a hard time to acknowledge its authenticity.

“They blew up the levees to save the rich and their fiefdom.”
“Barges laden with explosives were rammed against the levees on three different canals.”

“This happened in 1927, then in the 60's during Betsy and now in 2005, the history was manipulated again, a trifecta indeed.”

“That is not true” blurted out Tammy.

“Do you know anything of the great Mississippi flood of 1927?”
“Go read the history books white boy.” She mocked Brian.

She appeared confident that this white man was not a master of American history.

"History, sadly remain, not the absolute truth, but the montage of mangled half truths, a pastiche of the victorious." ranted Tanya.

Tammy took her hand and said “I am a social worker. We are just volunteers. I know what you must be going through, but it helps to talk about it just like you are doing now.”

Soothing words of wisdom seems to emancipate this anguished young woman.

Tanya burst out in to tears. She sobbed for minutes which appeared to be an eternity to Brian who kept shifting his weight.

"I am sorry for my outburst but, we have gone though a lot in the last few weeks.
This is Monica and she is five. She is all I have left."

As she watched the girl break away and run off to play with couple of white kids from the next bed, Tanya, with a smile, offered "she is the product of my partying days in high school."

Her grandmother was a proud woman. She made Tanya see the follies of her ways; give up drugs and made her go to college.

"On merit and not with affirmative action" she winked at Brian.

"I am at Tulane University this year, "she proclaimed proudly.
"Well that was before Katrina. Now I am not sure." Her forehead proclaimed furrows of uncertainty.

How could I have left? This time she looked painfully and near apologetically at Brian who looked past her.

"We had no transportation and my grandma could not walk far."
"The torrential waters came up precipitously and soon our only dry sanctuary was the attic."
"We stood in knee deep water with handful of food on the second floor contemplating the next move."
"Tanya, pull down the ladder we have no choice" she heard her grandma.
Even at her age and failing health she was in command.

“We were four women, Grandma, mom, my Monica and I. We were scared to death in the damp, humid and hellishly scorching heat.

“The attic was the size of a medium sized room. The pitch of the steeped roof made the room claustrophobic.”

“We had some food and water to start out with.
“Days went by as we clung to our dear lives in the carcass that was once a proud century old house.”
“Each day the flame of hope and fantasies of recue flickered unashamed against the backdrop of mounting reality of despair.”

“On the third day, we woke up to the cruel realization that we no longer had any water or food in spite of our frugal rationing.”

“In the fading twilight of that day my brave grandma breathed her last. Her sprit could no longer hold up the fragile body. She was smiling even in her death.”

“We sat for days with the mummifying body. Keeping vigil. One night my mother slipped away in to the swirling waters in the silence of the night.”

This was the tragedy of four American generations!

The afternoon was calm; she drove over to the dome. Jill checked on Tammy and Brain.
At the security check point Jill ran into to the same National guardsman, the young man who had joked with them on their first visit.

His eyes were sad yet hollow and distant. He had dark rings around those large emerald eyes that spoke of nights of insomnia.

“Are you Ok Guardsman?” Jill enquired with concern.

She had quietly noticed the ribbons he wore and was aware what they stood for. This was a decorated soldier. And was a veteran of both the Afghan and Iraqi wars.
She could see the emotional scars across his stoic face as he said" Yes ma’am I am alright Ma'am."

Jill in spite of her youth was a seasoned psychiatrist and could sense the intense tension that was radiating from this man.

"This was a person with PTSD" she said to herself.

“You come and see me sometime soon ok. I am a doctor” she did not want to mention that she was a psychiatrist in the earshot of other military personal because she was quite aware of the stigma that was associated with seeking mental health. It was viewed as a sign of weakness. Emotions were something that a soldier, sailor or marine took care of himself or herself.

All he said was "yes ma'am."

She knew that he had no intention of seeking help.

Joanne was spending another day at Crawley. She had mixed feelings about being there. She liked the people who she worked with but she missed the rest of the team.

Later that evening, in the comfort of the home, Tammy and Brian looked up the internet for the flood of 1927.
They found many articles.
What surprised Tammy the most was her own ignorance of the history.

Two of the articles that were succulent in her mind were the one she found in the national geographic by historian Stephen Ambrose written in the Expedition Journal and another one by John Barry.

The events surrounding Hurricane Katrina and the 1927 flood were similar in many respects.

Both, though almost a century apart, magnified the perpetual evils of the society. There was negligent lack of preparation, official apathy and incompetence, the class divide and warfare and racial inequalities.

Brian was dismissive.

"That was almost a century ago. I cannot be held responsible for that. I am sure that is not happening now."

"Brian, history repeats itself again and again. But the beauty of it is that that we are ground hogs frozen at 630am every morning."

“You knew all about it Brian, you have seen the demented patients."

"Besides it’s not all about you. You and I are just two pawns in the games they play."

Tammy had felt a sense of anger at the way Brian had managed their interaction with Tanya in a very unprofessional mode. She wondered what made Brian tick. Was he another Tom?

After dinner they sat down to talk about the events of the day.
Joanne had rented the movie “Crash”

She, Jill and Paul had planned to watch it. They had heard about it but had not seen it yet.

They had few drinks first and invited Brian and Tammy, who had buried their heads in the computer, to watch it with them.

They wanted to unwind after a day’s hard work. In spite of being trained in the mental health field and even with a few alcoholic drinks under the belt, they were unprepared for this movie and it’s after warmth.

Complete silence followed the movie.
Tammy had felt the loathing hands of the "Mat Dillon" cop prying aside her panties.

She was completely at loss what to do.
She felt used and abused.

“This is the most disturbing movie I have watched” she said quietly.

“She had it coming. If only she had followed directions." said Brian.

Brian stood up, ready to hit the bed.

“What do you mean Brian?" challenged Tammy. Tammy and Brian had spent a long day in the mirage of racial predicament.

Others, speechless, wondered if they had watched the same movie as Brian.

Jill called Dr. Higgins.

There was the customary exchange of pleasantries and then their flirty banter. They both felt that they were missing each other. They were longing for each other and their company. They talked at length about her stay in LA and he filled her in with the tales from the Burgh. He had to admit they could not match the intensity of the drama that was unfolding down south.

But,

Neither of them brought up the ghosts of PTSD!

CHAPTER 12

DAY FOUR

Jill made the Center her customary starting point in the mornings. The benefit of meeting and chatting with Jim and Andrea had a rewarding appeal to her.

She learned to avoid the hangers by at the front door. They moved away quietly making way for her.

They had grown respectful of the new, though young, doctor.

All her professional life she had to fight the stereotype. A woman in the medical field stood out as nurse and a male always a physician. This was the case in the eyes of an average person. This bordered on reality as the statistics supported this perception until recently.

Jim greeted her with the news of JC. He returned to the Center this morning because they did not find him a bed in the state of LA.

"They promised us a slot today. They are shipping someone to northwest hospital. " Jim stated with conviction. "Is he covering up for the shortcomings of his state and the mental health the system?" Jill wondered.

"Let the musical chairs begin again."

JC sat in the same cell san the bodyguard.

"He is no longer on the suicide watch and any monies scrounged by not paying overtime to the guard would be good money saved." Jim said aloud.

"He still needs inpatient hospitalization which remains the only way to guarantee continued medication for him."Jill cringed at the irony. Cost to the society would be more in the long run, just giving him the medications is cheaper.

They had started the treatment on Jill's

recommendation.

"Well, they at least did that for him. The hospital could have held the medications for another day punting back to the outpatient team to start all his pills." Jill explained to the students.

"The University medical center will not get paid for the care they offered JC during the last 24 hrs."

JC chatted away. His face brightened at the sight of Jill and her entourage. They found him less disinhibited with his outrageous comments today as compared to yesterday.

"You are back JC; at least they did not drop you off on the skid row like they do on the west coast."

"No skid row, however big, can hold me. They would have to kill JC, like they did big guy, to silence me."

"Certainly a difficult proposition to get a word in, leave alone silences you."Jill shot back.

"He certainly is less manic." She got one full sentence in before he interrupted her.

"They started you on Depakote, Tripletail and lithium yesterday.'"

"His medications are slowing him down." She educated the students.

"JC, how are we doing today?"

"Oh much better though I am not as creative as I can be."JC stated, mindful of the dullness of the mundane everyday life.

"Well, keep taking the medications. I hope to get you into a hospital bed today."

'I will Doc. I am bored. I don't have anybody to talk to."

JC was better but had miles to go before he slept!

Jill and the group moved on.

Jill enjoyed the clinical rounds she made with her students, quite contrary to the one she did back in the 'real life'.

She did not have long notes to write. No bullets or cheat sheets to satisfy the billing coder.

No fear of being the guest of the federal government in a white collar prison for Medicare fraud charges.

This morning she took upon herself to educate the students a bit about 'medical policies.'

"Historically most doctors worked hard on their patients but turned in poor records. At the same time, the bad apples among them, like the much maligned surgeon who played golf while his resident did the surgery, made life miserable for the honest majority. The Third party payer still got billed top dollar. Medicare lost billions because of this spurious double dipping (the Medicare already footed the lion share of graduate training.) "

"The way regulators demanded documentation to control this nefarious behavior, giving birth to the golden age of documentation, became the bane of all physicians. This cut tragically and dramatically into the actual face to face time. The only happy docs where the ones who made a living collaborating with the bureaucrat in making those pain in the ass regulations. None of it ever helped a patient or saved a life. These physicians wanting in their clinical or inter personal skills, found solace in those written words of wisdom."

"If something is not written it did not happen. became the mythological mantra. This repeated over and over in the hallways of the hospital made people accept the gospel until it became the truth."

This always brought a chuckle in Jill.

"If I killed someone but did not document. does that mean I did not kill him?"

"Writing longer notes meant more money."

"Even though the official line reverberated the billing to be purely on what you did, it always boiled down to what you wrote."

"A whole new industry grew to help the regulators and the 3rd party payors to support this wasteful habit. It just increased the overhead cost adding to bludgeoning cost of healthcare."

In Lafayette, Jill worked in a vacuum, away from those inexorable evils of modern medicine. Jill made a small note on JC's chart. It had all the required meat but not the bullets.

They spent time the seeing many of the regular patients of the clinic as well as some new ones from Lake Charles area.

Jill realized how sheltered her professional life had been so far. At the big house there is always abundance of resources.

She knew there was a shortage of doctors and especially psychiatrists in this country. Child psychiatrists could literally name their price because of the demand.

The few, not unlike other professions, flocked to the big cities and more favorable geographic areas to the chagrin of the poor and the rural areas. A state like Louisiana suffered the brunt of this scarcity even before.

She started to believe what Dr Higgin had taught her. Don't have to give the most expensive medication to make someone better. Sometimes the good old haldol does best!

She had her routine share of the chronically mentally ill. The regulars from the clinic and local catchment area got evaluated and treated by her. She also had patients who had been removed from their homes in the west.

She did come across a few first line responders now suffering from depression and PTSD.

No scintillating cases came her way but each of them had a story to tell. Dr Perkins and her students listened patiently, diagnosed and gave out scripts.

She would never ever meet many of them again.

Some of them, she wanted them to return before she left.

Amazed by the magnitude of the mental health burden, her appreciation and respect for Jim and Andrea, the unsung heroes of this tragic epic, grew exponentially.

She also realized that the drama after Katrina, made the suffering infamous but the Rita's victims suffered too.

"I am hungry."She called Paul. The two of them had been going to lunch together. Jill understood that Paul definitely enjoyed these breaks from the center. Being foodies, they experimented with different kind of cuisine, trying one restaurant after another. Jill gleamed some shades of Dr Higgin in Paul.

'You remind me of my mentor.'

'Is he as handsome as I am? Paul joked.

Paul became more relaxed with Jill as days went by.

Confident in each other's trust, they lowered their defenses. Jill gratefully remembered how Paul had dealt with her panic attack and flash back and also his tacit support when Dr Hodge tried to ride rough shod over her, her youth and her gender.

Paul on the other hand found his old passion, passion for work, life and maybe for the opposite sex.

He actually brought this up as he dug into a plate of fried chicken and dressing with buttery biscuits.

"Jill" He started to say looking up from the greasy fingers holding the crisp and spicy chicken breast.

He called her Jill only when they were alone. In company of others, Dr Perkins retained his form of salutation. She did understand why Paul did this.

Tammy addressed her as Doc. Joanne did the same like Paul but for different reasons and Brian used first and last names as he seemed fit in his perceived power play with Jill.

"Jill, I want to be frank with you. The last few days brought a spring back to my life. I have to thank you because this positive change is mainly because of you."

Jill feigned to blush.

"Mr. Maslin, are you trying to flirt with me, you old man?" After a few moments of poignant silence, both of them burst out laughing.

"One cannot fault me. look at you. I am sure Dr Higgn says the same." he looked at Jill in admiration.

Now Jill really blushed. She did like the approval from Paul just like she always glowed in Walter's presence.

" I have gone through a lot in my life, mostly good and a few bad. I am at a crossroads and I was not sure which way to go before I came here. I had become another paper pusher and I had lost the passion for the kind of work we do Jill. My family life too had suffered. We, my wife and I, became best friends and no more, the flame of romantic overlude long gone. Meeting you and spending time with you rekindled both."

"I am flattered"

"Do I have to sleep with you to keep the flame burning? You are not a bad looking guy for a dirty old man." Jill smacked his butt in fun and returned back to her jovial self.

They continued to laugh as they walked out of the restaurant and into their cars.

Jill headed to the Dome.

Paul returned to the center to do some didactics with the students. He would later follow Jill.

She enjoyed the short drive, which always allowed her to relax and think things over. She had to take care of her own life. Her life, in the middle of the storm, began to pick up tornado speed. She laughed about the lunch session with Paul. Paul and Walters were alike in some ways.

At the entrance she looked out for the Guardsman. She did not see him anywhere and then she noticed his friend from yesterday, the other soldier standing guard in the back.

She walked up to him and enquired about his friend. The kid appeared nervous.

"No ma'am Bill went home last night on short leave."

Maybe a bit of R & R might not be a bad idea Jill tried to reason with herself.

But the friend's eyes spoke differently telling her something was amiss.

Jill asked the friend Jim a few questions about Bill. Those questions, to the outsider would look quite innocuous.

Jill checked for any tell tale signs of PTSD.

Jim reluctantly gives bits and pieces and finally blurted out "I am worried for Bill"

"Why are you scared?"

"Bill has been different since coming back from Iraq."

"He is not sleeping well. Before, he would sleep through a bomb explosion."

"He is the coolest guy on the platoon but of late, he flies off the handle. The other weekend his wife Alice had a black eye. I asked her what happened and she told me she slipped and fell. I did not buy the story for a second. So I confronted Bill. Man, he was ready to skin me alive. We have been friends all our lives. He is different now. I can bet my life on it."

"What else did you notice?" Jill continued more than ever convinced Bill had PTSD.

"Did he ever tell you what bothered him?"

"No."

"Did he experience any trauma in Iraq?"

"Are you kidding me? That was one hell hole ma'am"

Jim had a hard time maintaining composure.

Both Jim and bill had their share of trauma at war.

It was a strange place for the two 18 year olds.

She had a gnawing feeling in her stomach.

She had seen many cases of PTSD.

There is more to this story.

But she could not put her finger on it!

Jill knew the cold statistics and medical data so well. She had recently attended the big conference on PTSD at Highland Drive VA.

"Over 2 million men and women deployed abroad to the combat zones since the wars began in 2001with half of them more than once and 6000 of them dead!"

"Military tacticians argue, compared to Vietnam, the death rate is low, but the price we pay is in TBI. The protective measures in combination with the degree of medical care has drastically reduced death toll,"

"The significant yet unheralded story is that at least 20 percent according to very conservative standards and up to 40 % according to some others, of vets are suffering from the invisible wounds. They have reported symptoms of the trifecta or a combination of PTSD, depression and TBI"

"Sadly only half of them with the symptoms have sought treatment."

"Many service members did not seek treatment for psychological illnesses because of fear for their careers and that it was a sign of weakness."

"But even among those who do seek help for PTSD or major depression, only about half receive appropriate treatment. Researchers estimated more than $6 billion as the cost to the nation as the result of PTSD and depression among returning Iraq/Afghan vets, they recommended a major national effort to expand and improve the capacity of the mental health system to provide effective care. The vets reported exposure to a wide range of traumatic events while they were being deployed including death of friends, injury to self or friends. Rates of PTSD reigned highest among Army soldiers and Marines. Women, Hispanics and non officers reported symptoms of PTSD and major depression more often than others."

Jill had been surprised how even the doctors questioned the validity of the diagnosis of PTSD. She has heard many a colleague claim PTSD was spurred by secondary gains.

"Trauma and its aftermath existed since time immemorial. In the ancient revered books it gets mention in the Book of Job and the Hindu epic Mahabharata. Throughout history, books recorded it in various forms. In 490 BC, during the battle of Marathon, a soldier got blind after watching the death of another though he had not suffered any physical injury. Spartan leader Leonidas and Ajax and Achilles in Homers Iliad came across the aftermath of trauma in the battle field. Later, it got mention in the Shakespearian plays of Henry IV Part 2 and Macbeth."

"Charles Dickens himself might be a victim of PTSD after a rail accident."

"PTSD as we know it had been called many names throughout the history until 1980 when DSMIII give the nomenclature".

"In Europe, among various nations, they had different terminology.The Swiss called it 'Nostalgia'. The German soldiers termed it 'Heimweh', and the French used 'maladie du pays', all of them meaning homesickness. In Spain it was called 'Estar Roto' meaning 'to be broken."

"Across the ocean in the civil war and post civil war time irritable heart was the terms used. In Victorian times the term used to be Railway Spine and 'compensation neurosis. During the years of WWI Shell Shock and during WWII and the Korean War 'Combat Exhaustion' described the same"

"DSM 1 in 1952 coined the term War Stress Response Syndrome and in the 3rd edition, the name PTSD was born"

Jill knew all this data and theory. She just had to apply the theory to herself in real life.

Tammy rounded alone.

Brian and she had decided to split their work load for the day.

Tammy went to the dome and Brian to the convention center.

Even though Tammy avoided the couple she had met before, she did not shy away from them. Maybe she was attracted to them sexually.

'.No way.' she scolded herself.

Brian on the other hand brooded at the center. As opposed to the dome, the convention site was dark and lonely, a brooder's liar.

Brian had dropped Tammy off in the front of the Dome. As she walked in through the checkpoint, she noticed the small bespectacled guardsman she had met before. The other, bigger man was absent but replaced by a woman.

Tammy walked to a corner bank of chairs and sat down to compose herself. Tom had not called after the first day. She had ambivalent feelings about the lack of response from him. Though mad at him, she missed him a bit too realizing her longing for the stability of American suburbia.

Her life sheltered and scripted in the safety of the Floridian suburb, until a few days ago, had reached a crossroad. Her marriage was not what she thought it would be.

She, with the help of her loving parents had blown 10k for the most wonderful day of her life, her wedding day. She had wanted it to be perfect and a perfect marriage to follow...

Tammy had the curves and a cute butt. She had caught Brian looking and admiring her behind on more than one occasion. She was not skinny but not chubby either.

Jennifer was an artist and she played the banjo. About Tammy's age, she had just moved to NOLA not too long ago and she had an eating disorder.

Jennifer was puking her heart out when Tammy found her in the toilet stalls.

She looked pale shallow and ashen Tammy thought.

"'Well let me call the Doc."

She got Jill on the cell phone and described Jennifer to her.

'I think she needs to be seen by the medical people.' ordered Jill concerned about the electrolytes.

Tammy marched the reluctant girl to the medical clinic.

As she helped the weak Jennifer into the clinic, three women, all of them comfortably chubby, looked up to note two young white skinny bitches and went back to their racist world.

"Excuse me I am a health worker and our doctor, Dr Perkins, think that she, pointing to Jennifer, and needs medical attention."

If Tammy had expected some positive response to the name dropping, she was in for a rude awakening,

"Oh the white skinny bitches who came by yesterday ordering us around?"

"Go sit down you all, we shall decide what to do" said one of them contemptuously.

Half an hour went by with the two white women sitting in the uncomfortable chairs.

Jennifer threatened to leave and Tammy had a hard time convincing her to stay while the three women sat nonchalantly on their well padded and appropriated behinds.

One leafed through the latest edition of Ebony, the second filed her nails and the third chatted on cell phone flirting with someone.

After an hour Tammy got tired and upset. She had noticed as time went by, this trio had helped many others who had come by.

Even the amicable Tammy could not help but notice that all those who came by were Afro Americans.

They were ready to leave as Tammy could no longer talk Jennifer into staying back.

At that precise moment two doctors, one woman and the other a male, walked in.

"We might get some help now."She stood up hopefully.

She walked over to the two with their quintessential stethoscopes tangling around their necks.

"Excuse me Doctors. I am a Tammy, a social worker, this girl needs medical attention." pleaded Tammy. She hoped unlike the not so helpful volunteers, the professional would be different.

The female of the duo turned and said.

"What do you want?"Tammy to her surprise sensed hostility in her voice.

"She has an eating disorder."

"Yeah that's all you skinny white women talk about while rest of the world starves. Why can't you two be like the sisters?"The male pitched in patting his colleague's ass.

All five of them, burst out laughing.

"There are better things to do." The two walked away. The male still had his big hands on the female's ass.

As she walked through the green labyrinth of the dome floor Tammy noticed she was staring at a patch of paint on the wall. It was a shade of red, not quite the shade of the lipstick she usually wore. She could not place the color from her past.

The convention center, a newer sister property, sat next to the more prominent Cajun dome and housed the refugees. Less crowded and noisy the halls and the main floor had a desolate look.

Brian was in a desolate place in his mind. This trip so far has been far from what he had expected.

Upstaged by a green horn female psychiatrist, he did not present the caricature of a white knight in shining armor he had hoped to be. Dr Hodge never held the medical profession in awe but he strongly denied any envy. The psychiatrists held more prestige and economic power over the psychologists. Brian believed the shrinks had better understanding and training than the drug pushers about the human mind.

In these dark halls Brian met Davis, an officer of NOPD, a decorated police officer.

After Katrina hit he had worked for the next two weeks living out of his car. His house with all his belongs was under water.

He came from an upper middle class white family. His father a captain in NOPD and his grandfather, a judge, represented the generations of "noble class".

After two weeks of harrowing and trying times he snapped. He brutally beat up a black kid who had broken into a store to get some drinking water.

Davis had enough. Repenting the morality of his behavior (lack of) or fearful he might have crossed the line and would find himself charged with Manslaughter, he just walked away from it all.

He got into his car and drove west and ended up in Lafayette.

Severely depressed, he self medicated with binge drinking.

Brian found him passed out in one of the dark corners.

He woke him up. Davis reeked of stale alcohol.

"How did you get the alcohol through the check point?"

"I still have my badge."

"You need to stop drinking."

He could not help a sense of loathing as he heard Davis's story.

Brian felt betrayed by a brother of his own race.

Without another word he got up and walked away from Davis who continued to drown his sorrows in alcohol.

Brian got a call from the Red Cross.

They wanted him to talk to this woman. She had cut her wrist, Now that got his attention. 'A borderline certainly.' he said to himself as he made his way to the first floor.

Joanne was at one of the smaller shelters at Crawley.

Crawley is a beautiful small town in LA.

They emptied out the shelters and in a day or two she would be done here and move back to Lafayette.

Joanne had spent the whole day at the clinic. They were very appreciative of her work. The whole clinic was talking about the International Rice festival. They wanted Joanne to come back and enjoy the rice festival.

She had to re-evaluate some of the folks she had seen at the shelter. As she walked through the small shelter, she came across a teen ager.

'Are you from mental health?'

'Yes I am Joanne. I am a nurse.

'I am Tim, can we talk in private?' said the teen in soft almost inaudible voice. He looked around at the same time, clearly uncomfortable. "Sure" Joanne led him to the room they had been using as her office.

As Joanne sat at the desk, Tim very meticulously closed the door, walked up to Joanne and came to rest close to Joanne.

Joanne had sensed the whole episode as quite strange.

Without saying a word Tim took on of Joanne's hand and placed her palm on his chest.

.

Now she was taken aback a bit.

She felt a human breast in flesh and in all its glory.

She instinctively pulled her hand back.

"I am sorry if I startled you."

Joanne focused on the loose shirt Tim wore. Yes she could make out a vague outline if she tried.

She looked into the Tim's eyes waiting for his story.

"Joanne I am Tim. I am a student at Tulane. I always knew I was a girl. I had undergone hormonal therapy and was waiting for the final surgery before the storm hit."

"Now here I am. I am not sure what will happen to me. I had psychiatric consultation and therapy before, so I am familiar with your services and felt safe with you."

"Things are ok here so far because it is a small place. I am glad I am not in a big place like the superdome, the Cajun dome or the convention center."

"We will see what we can do." reassured Joanne.

Tim thanked her and in parting coyly told her "you can call me Tiffany."

Jill walked through the Dome when Paul called her. She had seen and spent time with many of the regulars she had been following. Not a fan of drug companies, she appreciated their response. Her satchel remained a bottomless pit of medications.

For the hardcore psychosis she had medications like haldol from the clinic. The pharmacist would actually drive in with the medications. They did get hold of lithium in the same way for the manic patients. For depression and anxiety she had her collection of antidep meds.

"Jill where are you? Are you in the dome? I would like you to see someone here who might need medications. In fact make it two. I have a pair of twins with astoundingly similar stories."

"This is Mark and he is Luke." Said Paul, introducing two middle aged men with him.

Jill was a bit surprised because they did not look alike at all. Mark was white and Luke was black.

They had one thing in common. They fought together in Vietnam.

"Luke hid in the swamps of Louisiana and worked with the Vietnamese shrimp boaters on the gulf coast. He is ok except when the helicopters of the Oil rigs would fly over. He had flash backs and would cower down in the lower deck of the shrimp boats. The helicopters made him crazy. He should know he was a gunner on one of the choppers. He sat in the most vulnerable spot and had been in the cross wire of many snipers."

"He had become friends with an ethnic group that he fought decades ago. He lived with them. He would wake up with nightmares but they became rare until the hurricanes. He had a relapse with flashbacks and nightmares especially with the sound of helicopters. He cowered in a dark corner when I found him."Paul gave the thumb nail sketch to Jill.

Paul and Jill exchanged a poignant glance because both of them were reminded of the incident right here when Paul found Jill.

Paul continued his presentation of the history.

"Mark had become a drifter on his return from the war; His wife had already sent him the Dear John letter years ago. Mark was always a hot head, too quick to fly off the handle. This pre morbid personality did not help him on his return and combined with new found illness of PTSD, he got into trouble with the law."

"His string of bad luck turned on his first visit to Washington DC."

"Luke and Mark had been together in the war except for the last few months."

"Mark waited to return to stateside. He was the short timer. Then a month before Mark's time came up, Luke got shot down and they evacuated him to the hospital. He had lost an eye and his military days were over."

"Mark spent the last month lonely without his best friend."

"He also had a horrifying experience before he left south East Asia"

"They had lost contact on their return from the war."

"Strangely, they stood next to each other touching the Vietnam wall sharing the pain of the departed souls when they reconnected."

"The memories came flooding back."

.

"Mark, come to south with me. It will be like old times man.'"

"We can do some fishing, drink beer and the pot is good bro."

"Hey I have nothing tying my ass to upstate New York. And there is a VA anywhere you go."

"Mark agreed to join Luke"

"All his belongs and worldly passions were in his back pack so off he went to LA a couple of weeks before Katrina."

"Mark had a meltdown when they ran into Luke's new set of friends."

"But for Luke, who kept him tethered to reality, it would have ended in another travesty."

"Why the fuck did you not tell me you are living with Charlie (VC slang for Vietcong)" Mark asked.

"They are not Charlie they are my friends for over a decade now."Replied Luke

"They all are Gooks." 'Mark did not buy the story of redemption.

"Well let me get you a Ba Mu'o'i Ba (beer)."

"Over many glasses of beer and multiple weeds, Mark brought Luke up to speed."

"After you left something horrible happened."

"Do you remember the young hooch girl (Vietnamese women who worked in the army camp) in our camp?"

"Oh yes, how could I forget her." Luke had laughed out making his mime about her racks with his hands.

"Well we are not sure what happened. The rumors said, maybe one of the grunts (infantryman) got fresh with her. Anyway weeks later, she got a gun and shot up some men."

"I got shot too but lucky for me I lived to tell you this story."

Luke now understood Mark's lack of faith and trust.

Luke witnessed Mark's nightmare that night.

"He had woken up yelling."Don't shoot me."

"See I told you. They both have some symptoms of PTSD and maybe some medications can help." Paul finished the story.

"We can try different medications."

"I have some SSRi that could help. For nightmares I have used Prazosin but we are not going to get that here."

She gave them a week supply of Zoloft.

"Take one every day and let's see what happens."

She did not want to use antipsychotics ,at least not yet.

Brian went to the Red Cross office.

Two officials met him right away. Brian realized their non medical background as soon as they uttered their first sentence.

"She is from hell alright. We were going to call the police but thought maybe we should try you first.said the first official.

She did not apparently have much conviction in Brian's or mental health's abilities to control the riot.

"She is not that bad." chipped in the other drawing an angry glace from the former.

"What seems to be the problem?"

"She is the devil's discipline," continued the first. She is causing utter chaos to this place.

They proceeded to give Brian a short lecture on discipline and how the organization and this place needs to be run like a tight ship.

"She does not follow any rules."

"She fights with everyone. She flirts dangerously with strange men. She likes to be the center stage or else she gets angry."

"They caught her performing sexual acts. She comes back drunk and I am sure she does drugs too. I am sure she sells herself for drugs and money."

"And then she cuts herself."

"She is always threatening to kill herself."

"We cannot handle her and we want to leave her to the law."

The litany was stopped because they had brought her in to see Brian before they locked her up in jail.

She was a 20some girl. She looked younger like a teenager. She yelled, screamed and bad mouthed the Red Cross on her way in and at the door she announced to the world that no one cares for her and she planned to kill herself today.

"So tell me what's going on."

She turned her attention to Brian. Her whole demeanor changed and she became quiet. "Oh are you the doctor? I am so glad you are here. Please save me. They were going to throw me to the wolves. Oh and btw I am Mindy." she said in one breath and flirtatiously extended her hand to Brian.

Brian noticed her fingers lingered on his for longer than the social norm.

Brian was in his comfort zone.

This is what he did best.

He took care of the borderlines.

He spent time with her and in the end she became calm.

She agreed not to kill herself.

"Will you see me again tomorrow?" was her parting question to Brian.

After she left, Brian told them to call him rather than the police.

"We shall see." was the non committal reply.'

A new person sat at the table when they reached home that night.

Mary took Jill aside and said "Doctor we have a problem. I need a room for him. He is with the gas and Oil exchange and inspecting the area."

Mary never called her Jill.

"No problem. I will talk to the other two girls and we can come up with something."

As luck would have it, Joanne walked in through the door at the precise moment.

"Joanne do you want to sleep with me?"Jill asked loudly to the chagrin of Mary and a bewildered amusement on Joanne's face.

Mary tried to repair the perceived damage by explaining the tight quarter's situation.

"It's a king size bed."Jill explained.

"No problem. See you in bed lover." said Joanne winking at Jill.

Mary tried in vain to explain her B & B had a reputation to keep.

.

Jill and Joanne laughed at Mary's discomfort.

It would be true to say they felt a certain degree of sexual tension even though they were just kidding.

They both were heterosexual and never even kissed a woman in their lives.

After dinner the four of them had a ritual that went on to the dark hours of the night.

It started as a social event in the kitchen of John's and Mary's home, the usual supper and a glass of wine. They all had a glass. Jill and the rest always made sure there was enough wine. They would not impose on their host to provide that. They were doing much more than what was expected of them.

Even Brian joined in with his bottle of Perrier water.

They talked about world affairs or they brought up some local issues for clarification with the local experts, their hosts.

They avoided work related stuff.

They, the four of them Paul, Jill, Joanne and Tammy then moved with their alcohol to the patio and began their drinking sessions.

Jill knew she was drinking more.

She had started drinking a lot more after the death of Mike and it had become even more extensive when the nightmares started.

She knew alcohol did not help her cause but she self-medicated.

She admitted that she should talk seriously with someone.

"I will on my return." was her effort to quell her anxiety.

Paul, Joanne and Tammy all had their reasons for the "shots of medicine".

CHAPTER 13

DAY FIVE

Paul woke up tired.

In the past he had blamed the day time sedation and malaise on his sleep apnea.
Since coming to Lafayette he had slept well for a change.
He debated if this would be from sheer exhaustion of 16 hrs work days combined with alcohol.

Back home things had been different for a while.
Everything had become mundane and a chore, work, food, fun, sex, marriage and life in general.

He and his wife had grown apart physically and emotionally. They remained cordial, steering away from the perpetual fights.

They both were strong willed people.

"You two fight for everything just for the sake of fighting." their kids used to say.

The kids kept their consul during their childhood, but now they were adults and they had no problem voicing their disdain for the endless and meaningless arguments their parents had.

He had been contemplating to walk away and wander into the unknown. He had fantasies of leaving everything behind, the work, his family, the income and above all safety he had so meticulously worked for.

Maybe this is a way of suicide?

He had thought about self demolition too.

The methodological person he is, he had played the episode of his demise through suicide over and over in his mind. "Suicide can be made to look like an accident, only God and I need to know."

But as always, he conferred to life, more value than, the present day mordacity.

This reflected his existential dilemma.

He did not enjoy his current life. No he hated every second of it.

He had fantasies about an adventure through unexplored avenues and yet he clung on to the last morsel of organized life like the dying grasp of a man in self preservation. Working with the people here had an awakening effect on him. Jill, Joanne and Tammy had turned his life on it head yet again. He, a washed up older man, had a rekindling of life.

But last night he could not sleep. He kept thinking of his last half century on earth.
He took stock of his life; in the larger universal cadence his foot print had been significantly insignificant. He had chased material possessions but had nothing to show for it. The time had come for him to lose his moorings and set sail to a celestial world.

A mid life crisis Paul? He had questioned himself.

Paul did his rounds at the dome. He met Mark and Luke, the two Vietnam vets. They seem to be doing ok today with fewer nightmares and without any side effect to the SSRI.

Jules was a hit man or so he said. Jules brought Paul up to speed with a short run of his notorious criminal life in NOLA. He had for years, worked for the organized crime bosses in NOLA. He carried with him tales of havoc he had bestowed on many families.

They called him the Axe man, a throwback to the turn of the 20th century serial killer, the axe man of NOLA,

Paul didn't know how he ended up in Lafayette, but today, unlike any other day, he sought redemption by cutting his wrist with a straight razor like the original axe man.
Paul examined him after he had returned from the Medical center with a dozen stitches to his wrist.

"What happened to his mind?"
Maybe the weeks of misery had made him turn a new leaf.

What did the psychiatrists call this?

PTSD? Or Guilt?

The guardsmen brought Paul his next patient, an older gentleman. He appeared calm but somewhat bewildered. Paul looked enquiringly at the guardsman and they said.

"He was wandering around and we spotted him peeing into one of the trash cans. He would not give us any reason. He started to get angry with our questions and at one point pushed me. We did not want to lock this old man up as we figured he might suffer mental issues."

"What is your name sir?" asked Paul gently.

"I am John, Sammy my buddy, where had you been? I have not seen you since yesterday. I want to go home."

"Sure John, these men will take you home if you tell them where it is."
"Well that's the problem I cannot seem to remember the address but that is not important."
"What is your date of birth?"
"Can you tell me your social security number?"
"Where is your family?"
"What kind of work did you do for a living?"

All these questions met a stone wall of an irritable no.

After asking him to sit, Paul took the guardsmen aside and told them in a quiet tone."This is a demented old man here. I am surprised he had survived so far without getting hurt. I will talk to some people. May be he can be placed in a nursing home for the time being. Also let's watch him. We might have to work him up at the hospital to see if there is something else going on."

He picked up the phone to call Andrea. If anyone could make things happen in a flash, that would be her.

He also called Jill to enquire if they would take him into a medical inpatient bed. Paul knew it to be just wishful thinking as they continued to learn the ways of the world of resource rationing.

Jill returned the call from the Center promising him she would try.

Her next patient surprised her by not being a patient at all.

She introduced herself as a reporter from San Francisco, working in LA. She had been with the two, now famous Paramedics from SF, who had been in the center of a national controversy. The one claimed to be colored by racism in certain quarters.

She told them her Gretna bridge (The Crescent City Connection Bridge) story.

The incident took place on Sept. 1, 2005.

A growing group of people, stranded in NOLA without food and water, and some say at the advice of the authorities in NOLA, tried to cross the bridge from New Orleans into Gretna. This bridge spans the Mississippi River from New Orleans to Gretna and was one of the very few ways out of the water immersed city of New Orleans.

Officers with the Jefferson Parish Sheriff's Office, the Crescent City Connection Police and the Gretna blocked the bridge, turning the crowd back toward the Convention Center in NOLA. When some frustrated individuals in the crowd of mainly peaceful and with significant number of elderly and children, became aggressive, the Gretna police officers fired shots into the air and ordering them all back to NOLA at gun point.

This incident gained national attention because most of the police officers were white while most of the evacuees were black, and it quickly took on racial overtones.

3months later 60 Minutes story would "wonder why, under any circumstances, people trying to walk out of a devastated city would be prevented from reaching relative safety. It is inhumane to intimidate women, children, old people, and many on their last leg. But everything is not black and white, certainly not during these times."

(Years later the Obama Justice department would not file any charges against the officers.)

The citizens of Gretna, mainly white, wholeheartedly supported the Mayor, Police chief and the police department because to them, their lives and more importantly their property was at risk at the hands of the rioting black population ebbing across the bridge.
"I'm sure there are good people. There were scared and desperate people. And, unfortunately, contained within the crowd was a criminal element. This criminal element burned, looted, stole, threatened and terrorized," said Mayor Ronnie Harris.

The Police Chief Lawson had said: "We had no more to offer here than they did in New Orleans. We did not have food. We did not have water. We did not have shelters here."

"We did secure our community. I do not apologize for shutting the bridge down. You know my job and responsibility to this community was to make sure it's safe, the people and their property were safe in this community,"

People on the other side of the coin retorted that:" We weren't asking for food, water or shelter. We were asking for the ability to walk out of New Orleans."

"Just because you are stuck in New Orleans, doesn't mean you are a criminal."

"Unfortunately the law enforcement viewed ALL evacuees with criminal intent."

Many People expressed outrage that leaders of the society would and could say "Go away. I will not help you. You aren't worthy as a human being to be here."

"There is a limit to compassion. My compassion works only if my life and more importantly my property are not threatened." so they seemed to say.

Compassion fatigue was the name of the game in town.

But was it all black and white?

People initially crossed over. But 48 hours into the unfolding disaster, the media, all of them left, right, liberal and conservative rode the wave of hysteria and took the American population for a ride. American journalism in spite of the Pulitzer Prize was juvenile, sensationalistic and driven by the bottom-line.

All the major news outlets reported grossly exaggerated stories of heinous acts of murder, rape, and looting The Media as usual started it evil work of spewing their melodramatic untruth. The world population heard this over the radio and TV including the people of Gretna.

People of Gretna were scared too.

Media had to be blamed for creating such an aura of impending doom.

New Orleans had been one of the poorest metropolitan areas in the United States in 2005, with the eighth-lowest median income and with 1/4 of its population in poverty. Orleans Parish had the sixth-highest poverty rate among U.S. counties.

Poor people were generally viewed as of poor moral fortitude and the natural tendency seemed to be to always blame them for not only their own misfortune but also those of the people on the middle and lower middle class economic ladder.

Katrina not only washed away houses and humans but it also in ardently exposed the falsehood of generosity and humanity of the people, by tearing away masks and lifting veils of fantasy. The dirty belly of self indulgence was laid bare for the world to acknowledge.

Some initial reports of mass chaos, particularly in stories about the Superdome, later turned to be exaggerated or rumor. In the Superdome for example, the New Orleans sex crimes unit investigated every report of rape and found only two verifiable incidents, which would be not statistically higher for any given population of twenty-five thousand. They reported only 6 deaths at the dome and 4 at the convention center though out the trying times. They were all natural deaths except one OD and one suicide. In a case of reported sniper fire, the "sniper" turned out to be the relief valve of a gas tank popping every few minutes.

Clearly criminal activities took place but stayed a far cry from the reported hundreds of death and mayhem.

Fascinated by this account from the reporter, Jill made a mental note to pass this onto Dr Higgin.

Later in the day Jim called Jill.

"Dr. Perkins, the FEMA wants to talk to you."

"This is Mr. Watson from FEMA,"
"I want you to take some of your therapists on a bus trip to NOLA."

They planned to take buses with each of them manned by one therapist and no police or security on hand.

Skeptical by now, she was not going to take orders blindly.

"Tell me more about this plan." enquired Jill.

"We at the FEMA thought it would be a good idea for the former residents of NOLA to go back one last time and retrieve any personal belongings." said the pompous Mr. Watson.

"Why do you need us?"
"They might be distraught and might become aggressive so you could talk them down."
"It is what we at the FEMA want."

Jill saw hundreds of potential pitfalls to the plan and did not know where to start.

"I do question the plan from a safety point." Jill was getting angry at this dumb ass of a man.

No offence but Mr. Watson is you a FEMA employee?"

After a period of silence he said.

"Well not exactly….."
"Who do you work for?"

"We are contracted to do some work for FEMA.
"Well I do not take orders from you Mr. Watson. I will evaluate the appropriateness of the request and decide."
"Good day Mr. Watson." She hung up.

Brian at the convention center did not forget his daily tryst with Mindy his borderline patient. They spent time talking. The Red Cross had expected the mental health team to heavily medicate her to keep her under control. They were not too happy when Dr Hodges suggested medications were not the best treatment for this young woman.

He had in mind for her, a combination of Limit setting, consistency and a "make shift" form of DBT.

It seems to be working at least for the time being.

They had a new patient for him. His went by the name Ken. After an elaborate interview, Brian realized to his dismay, he was dealing with a man without any mental illness. Ken was just a sociopath.

After Ken left, Brian told the Red Cross official the news. "Please inform the police about this man's behavior. This is not a mental health issue."

This did not generate any verbal response from her but just a disapproving frown.

Tammy at the Dome ran into the couple again by accident. Tammy tried to claim ignorance. Her services honestly were not required because they didn't have any mental health issue. In fact they seem to be well adjusted in spite of their hardship.

"There have been studies regarding the etiology of PTSD and it has been shown that the pre morbid mental status, support systems before and after the trauma, plays a big role. Jill had told them.

It takes a village.... has not been lost to the researchers.

"People who had the support of the extended society seemed to adjust, recover well and though have suffered acute stress reaction, did not exhibit lingering or persisting PTSD."

They were making love in public and during the day in plain sight again!
Tammy, not startled this time, watched from the shadows. She was not ashamed to be a voyeur. She was not mesmerized by pornographic effect but by the tender loving making between the two, one thing missing from Tammy's young life.

Unlike the last time, the man, this time around, was going down on her. Tammy could only see his mane of white hair between the spread thighs of the wife who moaned softly. The rhythm of the enchanted moaning, without lyrics but with the fragrance of love and tenderness, was in the air. Tammy felt wetness between her own thighs as she stood watching. Her hand has a life of its own and soon she touched herself.
As the moaning grew so did Tammy's desire and excitement.
In a magical moment, not too much later, both the women reached the zenith of orgasm.

Crawley center wanted Joanne to see an elderly man who did not make much sense, the quintessential non complaint schizophrenic.

In poor health and unkempt, He was homeless way before the hurricanes and would continue to be long after Joanne would be gone.
He talked about aliens, conspiracy theories, the end of time and judgment day.

Mike, her next patient, also attained the label of homeless and just like our older chronically mentally ill patient before him; he too reached there before the storm.

The extent of the similarities ended there. Their history diverged drastically after that.

Young Mike was not schizophrenic and he made sense. He did not profess to aliens or conspiracy theories.

He had a name, a social security number, a job, a car and a family.
He lived on main street, USA as part of the establishment. Then one day on his return from lunch he found himself given an hour's notice and marched out. He had heard the stories about the corporate terminations but never thought it would happen to him. He learned his job was outsourced to India and his company no longer needed his service.

Months later, without another job and exhausted funds, he became homeless.
He joined the growing multitude of homeless people.

He had come down to NOLA because it is the poor capital of the world. People here lived on rice for a few dollars a day. The weather being hot, there was no need for heating, so living out under the bridges became bearable.

Months went by...
He got more despondent.
And then the surge of the hurricane carried him to Lafayette. He had talked to Joanne about getting himself on an antidepressant.

Back at the oasis, they talked excitedly about the next super hurricane Wilma.
This one seemed to be it heading straight for Lafayette.

Jill woke up from one of her nightmares. They had become more frequent now. All these months she had been waking up in an empty bed, but not tonight. Today Joanne was a bit startled at first because unlike Paul, she didn't know of Jill's panic attacks.

Not one word was spoken between the two women.

CHAPTER 14

DAY SIX

The day of Sabbath, unfortunately, was not one of rest for this lot.
They had their work and sheep to attend to. They agreed to start late though, a small mercy they allowed themselves.

Jill and Joanne decided to jog a bit. They ran along the streets of Lafayette immersed in their thoughts. Neither of them talked about Jill's nightmare. Jill stayed tight lipped and her buddy, for her part, did not yearn to probe.

As a silent witness to Jill's torture, she had picked up words "Mike", "death", "kill", "blood" and phrases please "don't shot", "oh my God no!' in the narrative of the nightmare. She also heard less familiar words like Piccadilly circle and Eaton.

She did not seek to dredge whatever painful past Jill had kept locked up deep inside her. She preferred and hoped Jill would open up on her own.

Mary, besides making her daily sumptuous breakfast, provided them a light supper most of the days.
The members pitched in to bring alcohol and deserts to join John and Mary at the table.

Evidently Mary did not render this service for money. SAMSHA paid the couple for their B&B, but these two provided much more.

They heard Mary prompt them to leave their clothes behind. She offered to do their laundry.

Joanne left for Crawley. She had requested Jill to go along with her. She wanted her to meet her patients and also give Mike his Zoloft. Their conversation touched on many things, their days here, work back home and Joanne talked about her children.
The two remained silent on the nightmare, Joanne mulled, quite unsure, how she would navigate the unchartered waters.

They started Mike on the Zoloft. Jill gave him a 2 weeks supply. The schizophrenic homeless man stayed in his own celestial world.
The authorities had finalized the plan to shut down the shelter and transfer the remaining to the Dome on Monday.

Joanne worried for Tim. He appeared to be safe here but the jungle of the Dome would be a mine field.

Jill joined her older colleague in seeing many more patients as the day dragged on.

In the evening, while at the stadium, Jill noticed the absence of Bill the guardsman and Jim his friend. Another detachment of National Guard with a woman soldier stood sentinel today.

Tammy, on a break at the Red Cross food service area, exchanged small talk with some members of VOA.

The Volunteers educated Tammy about them. They are a lesser celebrated organization than the more illustrious Red Cross. Tammy, like many Americans, had not heard about them. "They provide ministry throughout America. They had over 16thousand paid employees and another 40k volunteers in support role. Ballington and Maud Booth, the founders, in 1896, had a vision to create a sustainable organization for social reform. The pillars of this movement stood to help the needy all over America."

"Over the years," they continued the narrative.
"The Volunteers cared for people in poverty, and established the nation's first system of halfway houses for released prisoners. During the depression they ran employment bureaus, wood yards, soup kitchens and

"Penny Pantries." They served on the home front during both world wars. They operated canteens, overnight lodging and Sunday breakfasts for soldiers and sailors on leave. They provided housing and child care for defense industry workers. They led community salvage drives through the duration of World War II, collecting millions of pounds of scrap metal; rubber and fiber for the war effort. Volunteers of America had developed affordable housing complexes. They offered home health care and related services, including several nursing facilities, and assisted and independent living residences. Today, VOA is one of the nation's largest and most comprehensive human services organizations. They serve over two million people each year in hundreds of communities across the United States"

They have been wonderful throughout. Tammy had only good things to say about the VOA.

"Do you see that girl?"One of them said nodding in the direction of a guardswoman.
"A sweet girl but appears lonely even though she is not the only woman in the National Guard. The deployment had least six guardswomen here but she appeared different from the other five."

"Have you tried chatting her up?"

"Yes we have. She is always polite but appears distant with frosty glassy eyes. She does have pretty green eyes though."
"Ok I will talk to her." Tammy picked up two cups of hot coffee and walked towards the lone soldier.

"May I sit here? I am Tammy." Tammy always had a disarming smile that won everyone over.
"I am Jenna."

They talked for a long time. The conversation started as small talk at first but as Tammy got deeper and deeper, she discovered an ugly yet sad truth about Jenna. She was one among the many soldiers, both men and women, who suffered MST.

"MST (Military Sexual Trauma) is an experience, not a diagnosis or a condition in and of itself. Because of this, Veterans may react in a wide variety of ways to experiencing MST. Problems may not surface until months or years after the MST, and sometimes not until after a Veteran has left military service. For some Veterans, experiences of MST may continue to affect their mental and physical health, work, relationships, and everyday life even many years later."
US Veterans Affairs

Tammy, familiar with the sequel of MST, appreciated this trauma to vary from person to person just like rape in the civilian world.

This include acute stress reaction, depression, anxiety, insomnia, interpersonal problems at home and work, substance abuse to full blown PTSD.

Tammy, satisfied with the connection she made, called Dr Perkins to evaluate her for further management.

Jenna felt a big weight lift off her young shoulders. She had walked around in guilt and shame. She had not told anyone, not even her civilian husband.

Jenna understood the long road to wellness, a slow process of healing the silent wounds. But she was hopeful as she thanked her new found friend.

Brian, on his way to his daily therapy session with Mindy, stopped at the Red Cross desk to enquire about her. He was greeted by a different official today, a more accommodating one.
She informed Brian "Mindy is acting up again, threatening to kill everyone and herself. She does not mean any harm. She is just a poor lost girl. But others are not amused,"

Mindy's histrionic cluster B antics, did not sit well with them and they called in the cavalry to deal with the terroristic threats of our Mindy.

"This staff member is one of the" all good "people in Mindy current sphere."Chuckled Brian. He noticed the classical effect of splitting.

"Well where is she now?"
"She is in jail and on suicide watch."

Brian could not believe the idiocracy of the situation.

Adding oil to his flames of anger, the poor woman told him "They want you to fix Ken,"

"They think he needs therapy."

"What did he do?"
"He stole something but he claimed he had Kleptomania."
"Kleptomania, my foot!" Brain boiled.

Brian decided to educate the woman. But unfortunate timing brought in the other official at this precise moment.

There was no love lost between the two.

"Your friend is in jail where she belongs and why have you not talked to Ken?" accused the official.
Brain lost his composure at this juncture.

"You all are a bunch of fucked up idiots. You guys don't get it do you?"

To be fair to Brain, he walked away but you bet the story did not end there by any stretch of imagination.

They right away summoned Jill and she came down.

Jill totally agreed with Brian and backed him to the full.

She decided to be more diplomatic but stern never the less.

In the end they got Mindy out. She returned to the Dome with more daily sessions with Brian and the "Kleptomaniac" headed to the Jail.

As they moved away from this battlefield, Jill patted Brian on his back and said "You are the man Hodge! I could not have done any better."

Brian kept quiet.

In the evening, at the suggestion of the host and hostess of the Breaux Bridge B &B, a kind couple, who had come back to their native land to start this quaint B&B, Joanne recommended they go to the famous Mulante original Cajun restaurant for Sunday dinner.

They loaded into their cars and drove to Breaux Bridge. The packed restaurant had lively Cajun music with a crowded dance floor.

They sat down and enjoyed the drinks listening to the music.

"The various regions of Louisiana have different kinds of music. The east surrounding NOLA has jazz and the blues. In the west Cajun and Zydeco music rules supreme. The fiddle, especially two fiddles with one playing the melody and the other the second, are the original French/Canadian instrument. The German and the Bavarian accordion are later addition to the arsenal. The third piece is the triangle. The influences of the Texas country music, across the border, add the guitars (bass, steel, rhythm) and a drum kit, creating the popular dance hall Cajun music." Jim gave them a short intro to the native music.

Tammy enjoyed this outing, in her jeans and boots, she found herself to be the only one dressed to kill in her group.

The tall dark and handsome man came along and asked her for a dance and she coyly went along with him.
They did the usual Cajun jig but in the end he swept Tammy off her feet!

His name was Denis Cormier.

The group enjoyed the food while Tammy had something more than food and drinks this evening.
She had food for her heart for a change. She felt warm and tender in the arms of the mysterious Cajun.

Later, back home, they sat around the virtual fire, sharing the riveting day's fare.

Paul worked at the computer desk.
John, true to form in his role as the fabulous host, allowed them to use his computer after hours. They kept abreast with the outside world.

Paul laughed aloud which was sort of unusual for him. He usually is dry with his jokes and delivered them with a dead pan face. To see his whole body move, shaking with laughter, was a sight to behold.

“What is so funny Paul? Share with us.” They cajoled in unison.

“I think I would have to waste John’s paper and print a copy for each of you.”

"What are a few more papers for a good laugh? Look at all the papers the Republican Party sends me.” replied John.

Though a conservative, he did not shove his views down other's throat just because they stayed in his house.

Anyway they started to read…..

Paul’s friend, a psychiatrist he had known for years, had sent him a satire to unload his frustrations.

"The adventures of Tinker bell in the Never Never land."

Long time ago in the fiefdom of psychiatry lived a peasant psychiatrist.

His name was Tinker Bell, MD.

The psychiatrists, once the leaders of the clinician clan, and who the fiefdom was originally named after, had surrendered all their power to the present day rulers, the Demeanors. They in turn neutered and spayed all the shrinks and made the sorry bunch toil hard in the fields, caring for the crops and the live stock. In this fiefdom, the shrinks, devoid of balls and eggs, were treated worse than the street urchins when it came to hierarchical power. The Ladies and Lords lived off the sweat and blood of the psychiatrists.

Then one morning the Queen knighted him with the sword of Damocles, a folder of treatment plans.

The rookie knight started on the trail of the Holy Grail … in search of the peasant signatures on the sacred treatment plan. The most sacred of them all in the archives of Medicine Kingdom and holier than the Dead Sea scrolls! A bundle of papers, by decree, written in a dead language; neither he nor anyone with any degree of intelligence and certainly not the demented, could read, leave alone, understand, agree or sign.

Treatment plan, not a war plan, is a brain child of the Demeanors, the Overlords, in their valiant attempt to get their head around the concept of quantifying the inherent abstractness of psychiatry. Most clinicians, though fans of evidence based medicine, had a decent and adequate respect for the things beyond the graph able or graspable.

Thanks to the cookie cutter design of the powers to be, to validate, highlight and quantify their eloquent understanding of the latest treatment paradigm, they wanted transcending participation of all patients in the treatment plan.

With his life and those of the poor patients, hanging on the servitude to the mindless almighty, he set out to perform the gargantuan task.

He drove his entourage in search of this stupendous eight.

The first on his illustrious list-

Alden the munch

For a long time he reminded the shrink of the" hand" in the Adams family. But he is doing better, so he thought, though Alden remained mute.
Yes, he would be a good place to start.
He had a tendency to eat anything and everything offered to him or otherwise.

He is just an oral man!

Tinker Bell MD sat down with him asking him to sign the treatment plan. He looked at the paper, took the pen and paper from his hand and started drawing lines crisscross. "Oh he wants to play tic tack toe." Well Bell, MD obliged him until he decided to taste the flavor of the day by putting the paper in his mouth.

End of the plan A.

Alayna the catatonic

She sat outside in a belt to keep her from falling. Though waxy for the last 3 days, she sprang to life as Tinker sat down next to her. She snatched the paper.

The loss of control (of papers) scared Tinker because his instructions included "protect the scrolls at all cost."
She waxed
And then
She waned with her waxy flexibility and negativism.

But she would not let go of the paper.

Hours later, with a few shots of Ativan under her belt, he managed to prey the sacred scrolls from her hand.

Strike two

Two peasants so far, both refused/unable/needs more brain cells than just a couple to sign the treatment plan.

By now, all his apprentices had moved to safer pastures of academic grand rounds and he was left holding the baby.

Mother Alannah

She right away got into teaching him to be a good servant of God.
For over 10 years she had been trying to make a Born Again Christian out of him. After an eternity (at least it seemed to him) of her gospel teaching, he thought (wrongfully) she would listen to him.

He gave her the treatment plan with the same reverence he had shown to the rows of bibles and her own prayers she had published.

She solemnly looked at the paper, took a long breath, smiled and then proclaimed:

"I need to shove this up your ass BOY."

The shrink did not realize she meant it literally.

Until

She drove her walker faster and faster after him, shaking the scrolls in her arms trying to reach his behind.

Yelling Tally ho!

He escaped the torture because he still had a key to the kingdom!

Aldous el Demente

He calls the shrink babe as he does not sexually discriminate.

.
Aldous believes the shrink is his girlfriend and Tinker tries not to get groped by Aldous.

Aldous takes the treatment plan, rolls it in to a ball and tries to push it down the shrink's shirt, saying "I like bigger boobs….."

Well Bell MD manages to get away, again….

Algeron
He is on suicide precautions.
Bell MD gives him the paper but sees a strange look on his face. Tinker gathers the need for a pen to sign. The doctor is not sure if he wants to give him one because only last week he took a broken plastic fork and try to stab him.

Tinker realizes without some form of a pen, pencil or it's like; he will not be able to write.
Maybe he can transcribe for him, his signature...

Finally after a lot of deliberation, Bell decided to give him the pen.

After minutes, which seems ages to Tinker, while pictures of him stabbing himself and blood torrentially flowing out of his wrist flash through his mind, Algeron prints : "I do not agree with your F**KING plan. I want to die."

Algeron makes a daring act of driving the pen in to his forearm but Tinker is strong and ready for him. He stretched his arm, dived across the table and grabbed the pen in time.

Alanna the borderline

She was admitted last night and Bell told himself this is the perfect place to do the treatment plan.

They planned;

They planned;

And they planned a bit more.

2 hours later she wanted out.
It was nearing 1 pm.

Bell had missed his lunch break and his lunch as usual and it is time to run to his field (clinic).
At 1 pm they put away our dueling swords, called for her husband to come down from hundred miles a far...

On his way out.

He spied,

Alanis and Alton

To Alanis he proclaimed "Do thee want ECT? You sign here."

To Alton he said "Do thee want to leave this place? If thee so desire; sign here."

Alanis complained "There is no place to sign on the form."

He told her to sign anywhere she liked.

Alton asked Dr Bell "What am I signing?"
He replied " I don’t care, just *@#& sign!"

And off he went on his hurried way to his field.

Alanna part 2

After 530 pm, on his return from the field, Bell, MD and Alanna still worked like the congress on the health bill.

It was clear to onlookers that Alanna was filibustering.

“To sign or not to sign is the question.” Alanna flirted with him.

They spend another hour and half, this time in presence of her husband. He got her to stay but the treatment plan, still unsigned, and remained a work in progress after 3 hrs.

At 9 PM. Tinker bell MD on his way home, wondered "who is crazier, the patients, fiefdom or I?"

He reached his residence by 930PM.

"I am home."

……. and he replied to his wife's Dumb question where he was all this time.

"Honey it was another day at work!

They all laughed their hearts out.

They were clinicians, persecuted by the mindless minions who ran the establishments of mental profiteers. They could identify with the author.

"What is his name? Dr. Alfieri Albatross?" Enquired Jill.

"And the name of the hospital?"

"St Agnes hospital, Andalusia Alabama?" Jill was on a roll.

John had to ask the inevitable question.

"What is up with all these names that start with A? I am sure there are not this many people with the same letter for their name."

Jill laughed out.
"John, gone are the days when you practiced, life was simple then yeah?
Now we have to protect every bit of information to the degree of absurdity.

The politicians and the government know how to take a great idea and run it to the ground. They are good at making people's life more complicated for sure."

"We should get the government out of our lives" proclaimed Brian.
"You are right Brian, for once I cannot agree with you more" Smiled Jill.

"John, Paul's friend used the A****** word to name all. He tried to create this absurd pool of non existing patients and names to protect the PMI."

Paul kept laughing " There is more....."

"A funny satire indeed, but the response high lightened the absurdity further."

"He not only wrote this but he sends it out to many others on a Friday. The Bellicose fiefdom was ready for Dr Albatross on Monday to crucify him.

"The Albatross around the mariner's neck had become a royal pain in the cushy behinds of the pretenders of mental health."

Paul offered to give his friends a bit of the back ground.

He himself had languished in this department before he picked up and left for the plains of North Dakota.

Dr. Albatross knew, the litany of words was not in anger towards anyone, but driven by the apathetic moroseness of his professional and career progress in the department, something he thought, he had accepted and had came to terms with, a very long time ago.

He belonged to the group of physicians known as clinical educators.

They are a group of impotent souls living in their vacuous world.

Not driven by goals of scholastic pinnacles, they were even described as underachievers or plain money loving mercenaries by some obscure yet pugnacious academic.

The undercurrent of a desire to teach future doctors and an arrogant if not an egotistical drive to mould the young minds drove this bunch.

Though there is a certain dichotomy between the psychiatry department and the administration of a hospital, it is ever more perilous for clinicians because their lives and prospects were bundled together for them as they saddled the two. The department is perceived by clinicians as not caring for them and in their mind, they are considered by the department as an unavoidable blight and a tireless ass. It is unusual for the department to show respect for them because the perception is that of a pimp for the researchers.

The tortuous path for promotion was not worth their time.

There was never a feeling of belonging for them.

It is up to them to “carpe diem.”

Dr Albatross continued.

"I know my days at this place are numbered. I am not sure if I would end up getting kicked out or I would last until my last day. So I did not care a rat’s ass since I am flirting between a short timer mentality and random raucous, don’t care two hoots, behavior. I am at peace with both the outcomes for my future with department."

Tony kept warning him to be quiet.

Fernando said, “You and I are just mercenaries, the only bond holding us to the department is the money and they know the truth. They cannot run a brothel without whores.”

Colin said that a promotion (he has been offered the carrot many a times) is the worst insult for his work. And when they have nothing to take away from you, you have the power over them."

Paul knew Colin, Fernando and Tony. They had all been friends a long time ago.

Dr Albatross got private nods of admiration for his “courage to speak his mind.” While the abused continued to suffer in servitude. He did not even start to make any pretentions of his importance to this place. He remained a fly in the ointment.

He understood that it might be an unprofessional e mail he had disseminated. "It might have given me a fleeting moment of gratification, yes, you bet it did; and that's the least I could do for my own sanity."

Well that was the story of Dr Albatross.

"Thanks for sharing this with us Paul."
"I think I will be more outspoken after this"
"We all live our lives traversing the paths of least resistance. But is that really healthy?"

CHAPTER 15

DAY SEVEN

An overcast sky greeted Jill in the morning. The skies had been powder blue all these days.

Jill loved the sun though she lived in Pittsburgh. The city had a perpetual haze clouding the sunrays in the era of the steel mills. But, even today, the Burgh lacked Vitamin D.

Jill's two favorite cities, London and Pittsburgh, suffered overcast skies.

"Pittsburgh always had sunny the summers. The western Pennsylvania gets hot and humid with the needle often touching high 90's. This was in contrast to London's wet summers with a perpetual wisp of drizzle in the air."

She peeked out of the Tudor window in her room; and took in dull grey and doom. The weather reminded her of the London.

"Wow it might rain today. May be Wilma is on the way."She pointed out to Joanne.

A second night had gone by since they started sharing the king bed.

Brain made a big issue out of this.
"Your behavior is not professional."
The women's responded by completely ignoring him.

Mary had been uncomfortable from the beginning. She was the conservative catholic. But John laughed.

"Well Mary, do you think they are lesbians?"

Poor Mary blushed. She was such a textbook catholic!

Paul left for the Dome.

He switched places with Brian today. He enjoyed teaching and seeing the patients at the center. He began to appreciate the joy of clinical work without being hampered by the administrative chores that bogged him down in a swamp of medical records in the last few years. He had a spring to his steps.

Brian chose to enjoy a slice of down time after his run in yesterday.

He took over the teaching duties for the day.

The students would be exposed to a different style. Brian, a competent psychologist, knew his stuff, both the scientific as well as the inner clicking of the human psyche. What he lacked arguably was the artistic touch of healing.

"Maybe he has a shade of Asperser's in him" Jill wondered.

The entourage lead by Dr Hodges followed all the patients on the unit.
They, though impressed by his knowledge, sensed something amiss, maybe the humane touch, Dr Perkins so gloriously exemplified.

Towards the tail end of the rounds, he evaluated a police officer. The same one he had come across at the Convention Center. Officer Davis got intoxicated and threatened to kill himself. The LPD responded to the call and they brought him here to be treated.

Brian did a thorough evaluation and came to the conclusion that the officer was not suicidal but needed detoxification from alcohol.
In the absence of resources to do OP detox, he and the medical MD at the Center decided to admit him for a day or two.

He turned to the students, rhetorically stated with underlying contemptuousness, towards the man of law:
"What a waste of good life."

Jill took care of patients at the Dome and at the Convention center pinch hitting for Brian.

Tammy had seen Jenifer this morning. She had returned from the hospital. They stabilized her electrolytes.
She looked a bit better.

At noon, Tammy Jill and Paul went to lunch
The scene had been quiet and they had the time to drive out of the Dome/Conventional area to one of the neighborhood restaurants. They continued their parallel journey through the Cajun foodie trail.

Tammy came across the social worker Tanya and her daughter Monica.
They were yet to become their patients. They had chosen to keep away from the white help.

"Hey how are you?"Greeted Tammy.
" Where is the rude white man? Asked Tanya with a nervous laugh.
"I am sorry; I hoped to apologize to him for my nasty behavior."
"I will tell him you had been looking for him."
Tammy was relived because they seem to be recovering slowly.
Tammy continued her walk along the hallways of the Dome.

She contemplated the significance of the dance she had with the local man, the Cajun, yesterday.

"A bit fresh and flirty would describe my actions."
I had a couple of drinks." She introspected.

She enjoyed the feelings of excitement as his body pressed against her during the slow dance. She certainly got a jolt when he kissed her. She did not resist because the enchantment of the kiss had generated a fondue of love.

She also entertained a pang of guilt about Tom.
She realized he has not called her at all, but neither had she!

She remembered the color. The hue had been bothering her for the last couple of days. The shade of red. Then finally the connection forged onto her consciousness.

It was the shade of lipstick smear on Tom's shirt that had caught her eye while she did the laundry.

A tint she never wore!

The tranquility of the day shattered when Jill got a frantic phone call from Paul. The tone of Paul's voice surprised Jill.

"Come at once; the guardsman Jim is asking for you." the ever calm Paul sounded shaken.

Jill did not remember seeing either of them at the check post today.

She had gone in with Tammy and they had met Jenna.

After further conversation, Jill agreed with Tammy's original evaluation and recommended her to get some therapy through her work place. They did not think she needed any medications at this time.

"She is already looking better."
"You did a tremendous job with her Tammy."

Tammy appreciated Jill's approval.

Jill met Jim the guardsman and Paul in the clinic. Jill exchanged glances with Paul but did not completely fathom the expression on Paul's face. His expression reflected concerns for Jill's emotional health.

Unfortunately, she, an expert on human psyche, would not get the drift even afterwards. She remained blind to the inner working of her own malfunction.

Jim looked profoundly shaken.
Before Jill had time to sit down or share pleasantries, Jim blurted out.
"Doctor, Bill is dead!"
"What?" Dr. Perkin heard herself say.

She noted her heart beating faster and a sense of constriction around her chest. She perceived a lump in her throat and perspiration on her cheeks and the hair on the back of her neck stood erect.

She took a deep breath and ploughed on.
"Tell me what happened."

"As I told you, few days ago, when I met you at the check point, Bill had gone home on short pass."

Then out of the blue Jim started crying. Torrential tears rolled down from his eyes.
Jill sat with Paul in silence.
Paul and Jill looked at each other and nodded in agreement.

The time had come for the 18 year old kid to let go of the stoic military facade.

After few minutes which seemed like eternity, Jim, wiping his tears and regaining composure bellowed in a regimental voice "I am sorry sir. This will not happen again."

Jill took his hand and in a soft tone said
"Son, it's ok."
They sat in silence for some more time.

Finally;
Jim began to tell the story.

"I think I made an error by not telling you everything before." he stated sheepishly.

"I am educated on the silent injury, I am sure Bill had PTSD."
"I should have told you Doctor, but I did not want to snitch on him."

"It's ok we all do that Jim" said Jill patting the boy's arm.
Jim took Jill's slender hand in his and gently squeezed it, smiled and continued his narration. He held on to Jill like a

child hanging on to his mother's comforting and protective hand.

Bill had shown evidence of stress since they returned from Iraq. He was a changed man. The qualities of Bill, everyone in the little town loved, had disappeared.
He had been the life of the party but now had become isolative and brooding.
Jim and Bill had been friends all their lives. They came from a town in northern LA called West Monroe, an archetypal small town USA with a population of @ 14k, on the banks of river Ouachita.

They lived on the same street.

Their dads worked in the gas line Pipe Company. They went to west Monroe high school and both joined LA National Guard, a highly decorated organization serving admirably in Iraq and Afghanistan. At home they had been the backbone of the national guards' efforts following the hurricanes.

Jim said Bill's wife had reported sleepless nights for her husband along with nightmares.
Jim admitted Bill had been drinking heavy which he thought was because of the problems with his wife.

Bill had become short tempered and irritable.
He completely avoided talking about their experience in Operation Iraqi freedom and stayed away from all his friends.

He had a few run in with officers, but given his decorated history of 2 purple hearts, that was swept under the rug.

Jim had experienced at least one episode of flash back in Bill.

Bill, since his return, sat with his back to the wall.

The National Guard had got him into treatment and everyone looked away.

"I should have known better. Bill is a proud man. It is not easy for him to show weakness."

Jim re told the story about the bruises on his wife.

Last week Bill had dropped the bomb and left for home.

Then he heard that

Bill shot and killed his wife and child and then died by "suicide by police." in the ensuing standoff.

"What did Bill confide in you Jim?" asked Jill.

A pained dark cloud crossed his face.
Jim hesitated not sure if he wanted to share the deepest secret with two strangers.

"We are all professionals here Jim. We will treat whatever you tell us with utmost respect and privacy as possible." reassured Jill and Paul nodded in agreement.

"Well it's hard me to tell you the story."

"Bill had a hard time sharing it with me. I don't think he even told his wife or anyone else. I knew he never divulged this inner most secret to his therapist. I had told him to, but instead went on to….."
His voice broke up and trailed off.

They gave him time. He needed to narrate and unload this story on his own terms.

"Bill became a troubled man inside since he returned from Iraq. He was torn within. "

"This is the story he shared with me the last time I met him."

Bill was on guard duty at the base one day. In the fading light of a desert day, he eyed a car speed towards the gate. He walked across to the middle of the road ordering the car to stop but the car continued to move towards the gate at a fast pace. He did everything in the book to stop the car to no avail. He had to do what he trained to do.

The shooting ended and the car came to a stop.
A bloodied man stepped out of the car.
"Oh no, I know the man "Bill had a sinking sensation inside him.
The man said nothing but had the look in his eyes that seems to plead:
"What have you done my friend?"
And behind him, his wife and two kids, lay dead riddled with Bill's bullets.

"Kadar had been the station electrician for years.
On his day off, he was taking his family to the movies when he got the call. There had a malfunction in the water

heaters and one of the soldiers got electrocuted and they wanted him on the base ASAP. He was only a few minutes from the base."

"In a frame of mind, shaken up with the sudden death of a soldier he knew, he had been juggling with and looking at his pager and the cell phone against the back drop of the incessant cries of his baby and the nagging questions of his irate wife, he just did not stop."

"Everything had happened so fast in the fading light of the dusk."

"The tragic episode underwent extensive investigation and naturally Bill had not done anything wrong but for him this made him a monster in his mind.
"He told me he could not sleep; the face of the electrician remained crystal clear in every moment of his life."

"He returned to west Monroe to a hero's welcome. He was a true Hero to the town and the country but he perceived him to be an evil man."
This existential battle ravished in mind and psyche and I think he just went crazy."

"Jim I think you are having a hard time. I am ordering you back to your brigade to seek help."
Jill decided to be stern.

She, like Jim, wondered if Bill would be alive if they had acted...

"What a story. Who could have seen it coming?" Paul tried to deflect any self doubt she might harbor.

They walked towards their cars.

.

"Are you kidding me Paul? I should have seen it miles ago. My gut told me something was wrong on day one. I should have pulled rank and called his commander."

"At least we did the right thing with Jim." Paul tried.
Nothing is going to bring Bill back." retorted Jill.

Jill began to breathe hard, sweat flowing down her back and her blouse drenched in sweat of self depreciation.

She stopped talking and stared off into the distance.

"Are you Ok?" Paul enquired of Jill.
"I hope so" she replied.

"Do you want me to drive? We can pick up your car tomorrow." Paul offered his services. He asked with concern.

'I will be ok Paul, thank you anyways." she squeezed Paul's arm is appreciation.

Paul knew better than to argue. Jill is stubborn. He so wanted to hold her and comfort her instead he planted a light kiss on her forehead and walked away saying:
"See you at home Dr Perkins."

Jill sat in the driver's seat. Her hands trembled.
"Steady yourself girl" she said aloud.

It was getting dark. The whole day had remained dreary. It had been a long day for her, a sad and traumatic day. She knew in her heart. "It was her fault that Bill is dead!"

No matter what her brain told her, she began to believe what her heart said.

Jill realized she was losing control of her life.

She had insomnia.
She drank more than she should.
She had daily nightmares of death.
She was getting short tempered and having difficulty with concentrating on task at hand.

She had distanced herself from Mike's friends and anything connected with the military to avoid any kind of memory of the trauma.

She jumped headlong into her work and she was glad that her routine work at the big house did not include trauma. She treated depression and little old demented people.

Even then, the symptoms got worse.

She should have talked to Dr Higgin but she kept putting it off. Then the opportunity to work in LA came. She foolishly grabbed it thinking this would be like exposure therapy.
She had been able to hold it together because of the challenges to the job but she felt drifting like a boat that had lost its mooring.

Today was different. The old wounds had reopened.
She had failed Bill.
Jill, as she stared past her pale knuckles on the steering wheel, saw the images of Mike and Bill.

Both of them smiled at her and then at each other.
Their faces danced in the amber glow of the setting southern sun.
They merged into one entity.
The thundering subway collated with the speeding car.
The echoes of the tube shattered the cacophony of M16 rapid fire.
Checkered turbans danced in their flowing white gowns.
Mike lay dead beside the Mercedes, shot up by Bill's gun.
The electrician pleaded with the subway ticket collector for mercy.

She started her car…..
Driving the car towards the check post, she saw Bill shouting at her.

"Stop the car now!"
She heard him but powerless to stop, the car picked up speed.

She was going to drive herself in to the devil.
She saw Bill raise his gun.
He pointed it at her head.

She heard Mike Plead.
"Jill stop the car; stop the car!"
Please stop the Car, Bill pleaded too.

But it is too late.

The gunfire shattered the windshield.
The noise grew louder and louder in Jill's ears.
Blood splattered and covered her face clouding her vision.

STOP! STOP Jill!

Paul sat in the passenger's seat holding the key.

Paul had stayed back to take care of Jill. She had just experienced dissociation and flash backs again. As the shadows of the evening elongated on the empty parking lot, they sat in silence. The guns, the cars, the tube, the terrorists, Bill and Mike were all silent.

Brian regularly called his mother. She is elderly and as a dutiful son he always checked on her.

He shared his experience with her.

"Mother I ran into a Lebanese girl today." Brian was telling her the story of one of the medical students he had met today, she was not a beauty queen but what was striking about her was the eerie resemblance between her and Brian to the point it was unsettling to him.

His mother chuckled "It is not too farfetched."

"What do you mean mother?"Brian asked startled.

"That you two could be related!"

"No way! Stop teasing me liked that. There is no way I could be related to one of them."

"I am white. He completely believed in his race in spite of not having blond hair or blue eyes.

Brian had researched the family tree long time ago.

He was proud to be a Saxon.

The first Hodges was Saxons in England, even before the time of the Norman Conquest. After the fall of the Roman Empire, the Saxons, who were fair skinned people from the Rhine valley, arrived in England. They settled in the county of Kent, in southern England. During the next four hundred years they ruled the south.
The Normans from France invaded England and occupied the Saxon land following victory at the Battle of Hastings in 1066. Some of the Saxons moved north.
The Hodges emerged as an influential name in the county of Northumberland.

The New World offered better opportunities and some migrated voluntarily during the later centuries. They sailed aboard the huge armada of sailing ships. They are amongst the first settlers in North America. From the port of entry many settlers went west, joining the wagon trains to the Midwest and then some on to far west.

"Brian it does not matter, your dad and I are Mennonites.

"That's why I joined the born again church."

Brian never agreed with the religious practice of his father or mother. He was even more foreign to their social philosophy.

His mother hoped, as time went on, he would become less of a right radical and more of a middle of the road person.

They did not support war and believed in taking care of the poor and the needy. They actually practiced what they preached.
Brian was just the opposite on his racial views, and social philosophy.

"Let me tell you something I have not told you before." His mother sensed the time had come for him to be enlightened about his origins.

"I know you always wondered why you had dark hair eyes unlike Saxons of Rhine valley." said his mother with a mischievous smile.
"Why?"

"Because you are not a Saxon"
"What. You are kidding me?"

"My father was a Hodges; I researched the family tree."
"No, my child. The man you call dad, was my husband but not your father."

"What, do you mean?"
"I maintained that I was pregnant when your dad died. That was a lie.
Dr. Hodges, my husband, died in the car accident, before you were conceived."

"My husband and I had a very close friend in Africa. He was Lebanese. In the months following the tragic death of my husband we became even closer….."

"You mean I am Lebanese?"
"Yes your father was Lebanese so you are part Lebanese."

"The irony of you landing in Lafayette LA, one of the better known areas of Lebanese American history had not been lost on me."

This was the most dramatic day of his life. Everything he believed in and was beloved for him had come crumbling down….

"You are in the company of some famous Americans who had some Lebanese blood in them." She was very active in the Lebanese American communities and new facts on them.

His mother was enjoying this moment in her dying days. She rattled off the names of some famous Lebanese Americans. All of them had some shade of Lebanese heritage in them.

Michael Elias De Bakey, the world-renowned cardiac surgeon.
Helen Thomas – journalist who covered every U.S. President from 1961 to 2010.
Christa McAuliffe, the American teacher from Hampshire, who was one of the seven crew members killed in the Space Shuttle Challenger disaster.
James "Jabby" Jabara, the first American jet ace in history.
Robert Khayat – chancellor of the University of Mississippi.
Actors Tony Shalhoub and Vince Vaughn.
John J. Mack, CEO of investment bank Morgan Stanley.
Paul Orfalea, founder of Kinko's.
George J. Maloof, Jr., businessman and owner of the Sacramento Monarchs, Sacramento Kings and the Palms Casino Resort in Las Vegas.
John Zogby – founder, president and CEO of Zogby International.
James George Abourezk and John Edward Sununu former United States Senators.
Edmund Spencer Abraham, a former United States Senator from Michigan. He served as the tenth United States Secretary of Energy, serving under President George W. Bush. Abraham is one of the founders of the Federalist Society.

Raymond H. "Ray" LaHood a Republican politician from Illinois.

.

"Doug" Flutie the quarterback.

And don't forget your Local Lafayette man Kaliste Saloom.

And of course the one and only Ralph Nader!

Jill called Dr Higgin
She knew she had to call him.
She described what had happened with Bill.
They launched into an academic discussion whether you could develop PTSD when the trauma, that is the root cause of the anxiety disorder, was perpetuated by the patient himself.

"I am not sure the picture fits the DSM diagnostic criteria."
"May be its guilt." Well let's go over the DSMIV criteria for PTSD."
They both brought out the pocket version of the DSM IV and looked up PTSD.

309.81 DSM-IV Criteria for Posttraumatic Stress Disorder.
They went down the list of Criteria.

"Let's look at the criteria as applied to Bill your national Guardsman."

I know A (1) is controversial, so let's put it aside for now." prompted Walter.

He did experience horror and helplessness A (2) at the time of the event.

Jill went down the list.
B: "Recurrent re experiences of the traumatic event. "
Even though I did not obtain a direct history from Bill, I have pieced together one suggestive of re experiencing the "trauma" directly or symbolically."
"I am sure he had intrusive thoughts, recollections, hallucinations, flashbacks and nightmares."
C: Avoidance: "Clearly he was a changed man in his relationship to the Town and its folks and speaks strongly of his avoidance.
D: He had symptoms under hyper arousal, insomnia, and anger.
E: Yes, it had been longer than a month.
F: well he is dead! How more dysfunctional can you get?

"So he had the symptoms of PTSD but does the stressor A (1) qualify as criteria remains to be seen." Jill submitted.

"Well, there was a traumatic event resulting in the death of people he knew (wife and children of someone he knew), and at that time or soon after the event he did feel helpless." was Walter's analysis.

"You can make a case but will not fly with APA because he was the cause of the trauma." he added.

"Story might be different if he did it premeditated.
Here he was an unwilling perp." Jill brought up that facet of life where people do heinous things that are beyond their control.

"Like,
a father or mother or sibling forced at gun point, to rape their child or sibling by the rapist in a home invasion or carjacking?"

"How about an accidental death caused by a person?"

"A hit man, who killed many, later experiences an epiphany and the symptoms of PTSD?"

"Would he qualify for that diagnosis?"

"Or do we decuple the criteria A from the rest?"

"Anyone with the symptoms (B through F be called a generic name like anxiety disorder NOS or chronic stress disorder (already an acute stress disorder exists) or chronic adjustment disorder severe?"

"Only who qualify for a stricter and narrower definition of A should have PTSD?"

"This is clearly a case of cause and effect. You have none in some of the disorders like panic disorder or phobias. We all face adversity in our daily life. When, how and in whom, it rises to the level of intensity, to be defined as a trauma, is debatable and maybe individualized and it might never be able to actually be pigeon holed."

"Then there is always the question of money that underlies it all. The US government took a long time to recognize and compensate the vets."

These were all good questions in the academic discussion the two were having.

Was this a moral injury?

Jill said that she sensed certain degree of guilt because she could have intervened.
Walter knew that no matter what he said, she had to work through that perceived guilt.
"It is not uncommon for doctors to appreciate guilt and inadequacy when something bad happens to our patients." Walter said.

"You are not God Jill!"

They were still dancing around the much more intimate issue of Jill's mental health.

Jill underplayed her experience in the parking lot.

"Jill, I think you are having a touch of PTSD yourself"

"No way! No trauma to me and DSM IV says.....

"Can not accept trauma by proxy; she was referring to the death of Mike."

Fuck the DSM." was Dr. Higgin's reply.

"Maybe the unexpected and traumatic death of Mike itself was the trauma for you Jill."
"Please I want you to take care of yourself."

Walter was torn between patronizing or condescending and ignoring the tell tale signs.

He was quite wrong wasn't he?

CHAPTER 16

DAY EIGHT

They were at midpoint of their tour of duty.
"An interesting stay so far" appeared to be the overwhelming verdict.

Paul went to the Center looking for Jim and Andréa. He planned to discuss our John Doe who didn't remember anything except his given name. He is an urgent case for placement. They tried hard to place John in a supervised setting, at least until someone claims him. It certainly was a miracle how he had survived until now.

The police, the Red Cross and the VOA were aware of the mental capacity of the John Doe. They kept an eye on him and so far they had been successful. None of them took any bets on how long the honeymoon period would last.

Andrea had good news. She found a place for John and they would accept him soon.

"You continue to amaze me. What tricks did you pulled out of your hat for this Andrea? "Paul thanked her in admiration.

Today happened to be the day the other shoe dropped. The guardsman at the check post recognized Paul. "Doctor, there are some new developments." he filled in the details.

Early this morning our John became belligerent after he stumbled into an altercation with someone after he evaded the watchful eyes of the VOA.

The event started with John accusing a young man of stealing his shirt. This of course wasn't true. He kept following him pulling on the garment. To the credit of the youth he walked straight to the police. Before they had time to intervene, John called him names and punched him on his nose.

John faced assault and battery charges. The police, aware of the mental health team presence at the dome, held him awaiting the expertise of Paul.

John completely denied the episode.
He had no recollection of the shirt, the man or the altercation.

Paul took charge of the situation.
Jail certainly would not be appropriate for this poor guy. He wanted to hospitalize him for a couple of days before sending him to the home Andrea had wrangled for him.

He called Jill to explore possibility of hospitalizing him. In the mean time he turned to talk to the Afro American man.

In spite of a bleeding nose, he found the kid in good spirits. He cut short Paul's attempts to explain the behavior of the old man.

"I should have just run away. He is not all with it in his head. My grandfather had Alzheimer's, so I do understand." he laughed.

Brian happened on the old lady sitting in a rocking chair with her dog. As he walked up to her she looked up at him with sad puppy eyes and said.

"I don't know why he would not drink."

Brian had a hard time suppressing his laughter. The dog actually was a stuffed animal. He saw chocolate milk running down the side of his cotton mane.
He sat next to her and asked.
"What is your name ma'am?"

"Mary and this is Patches pointing to the dog. He is my only friend."

Patches was an aptly named Chihuahua.

"Well Mary, I am glad Patches did not like chocolate milk, it would kill him. Dog hearts can't handle chocolate."

"I am so happy then." she pledged ignorance.

"Mary, I don't think we need to feed him. Promise me you will not until he asks for food."

"OK I will do that. He talks to me."

Brian did not want to challenge this old lady's delusions. It would not serve any purpose besides the animal albeit not a live one, remained her only companion.

He squeezed the frail hand and moved on.

Dr Perkins was having a busy day at the Center with a schedule full of patients.

Many of them had depression and required treatment with medications. Others suffered acute stress reaction from the hurricane experience, first responders and victims, alike manifesting varying shades of PTSD.

The usual SMI case load also made their mark, people with schizophrenia and similar chronic illness who needed the regular medications. They had lost the scripts, records, therapists, case managers and MDs in the hurricane.

The phone rang off the hook for Jill.

Paul presented the case of John Doe. She concurred with Paul. She preferred a dementia work up on John before diagnosing it dementia with anterior brain dysfunction," He might be delirious too and maybe both are present."

She did not want to miss the boat because the underlying cause of delirium would be treatable, and that if not treated, might turn fatal.

Also John may have some treatable causes of dementia.

The university hospital did not appear generous.

"Did we not talk about him before? He is just demented."

"Yes and we had him under observation. He acted out again. This might be pure baseline dementia but we would be practicing poor medicine if we don't check for other etiology. There isn't any outpatient resource to work him up."

"Well do you want me to waste a hospital bed?"

"Do you want me to send him to jail for his actions? Jill shot back.

Amazingly, even the medical field was uncomfortable dealing with the demented and their behavioral dysfunction.

"They agreed to accept; Paul. Have the police escort him to the University hospital." Jill called Paul back to update him.

"Thank you Jill, You are the man."

Next on the phone, Joanne surprised Jill. Joanne sobbed at the other end.
This was out of character for Joanne.

"Calm down girl. What is going on? "
"I got a call from my husband. He wants a divorce."

He, without much ado, told her he was leaving her for this young beauty he was madly in love with.

She had her suspicions about the philandering spouse but she would not admit to herself or even challenge him.

She had noticed those receipts in his suit pockets that did not add up.
She had been in denial so far, but now hit with the truth, her world was spinning out of control.

"He does not deserve you Joanne."
"I feel like a total failure."
Let's talk tonight Hun."
"Oh Jill."Joanne had forgotten to mention." they would be moving Tim to the dome."
"Will you check on Tim for me at the dome? I am scared for him."
"Yes I will try to track him down this evening."
"I will tell him to ask the VOA or Red Cross for you."
That's a good idea, you do that." Jill hung up.

She completely forgot to check on Tim, as she had gotten extremely busy at the Dome later in the day.

No one came looking for Jill either.

Tammy phoned her soon afterwards with more drama.

Tom had finally called her. He demanded her immediate return to Tallahassee. Tom's egocentrism would not accommodate the fact she could not just pick up and leave.

"Tammy, you get back right now."

"No, Tom I cannot do that. I have my responsibilities."

"You little tweet; your only responsibility lies with taking care of your husband."

"Says who?"
"Says I, and the bible." Tom like any good hypocrite used the good book and the Lord's words to manipulate.

"I am not coming back, not yet"

"That is peachy, well then you stay in LA for good. I am sure you will find some Cajun redneck to fuck you, you slut." Tom slammed the phone down.

Tammy's reaction and response pleasantly surprised Jill. Like a rock she remained calm and matter of fact.

"Two can play this game. I will look for my Cajun red neck then." She laughed.

Jill could not but help join in the laughter. "Tammy, hey girl, you have come a long way."

Both the husbands had called at the same time with their "dear Jane" letters.

Jill did not leave for lunch as usual. She told Paul to go ahead without her.
She sat in her office brooding….

She had been holding together pretty well or she thought. Her fray into this world was a muted attempt to treat her problems associated with the trauma of Mike's death, doing exposure treatment on herself.

She was aware of the fact many mental health workers make the mistake of treating themselves.
"I can handle it." had been her mantra all these days.

She acknowledged her alcohol intake had increased significantly which she rationalized to be due to the intense work they were doing here.
"I will scale down to my usual rate of consumption once I go back to Pittsburgh."
A small voice inside her challenged this .The increase predated the trip but she conveniently chose to ignore the truth.

She became depressed though the rigors of the current job.

She lost her zest for life, and things were not as delightful as they seemed before.
She also had poor sleep, concentration and she sensed certain elements of irritability in her.

She called Cynthia McAlister.

Dr. McAlister was the chief resident and a good friend of Jill. Jill had been her chief when Cynthia did her internship. Over the years the two women had forged a great friendship and they did share their experiences.

. "Yes Dr.JP, how is the deep south treating you?' In spite of their closeness, Cynthia always called Jill Dr.JP.
'I am ok."

Cynthia, not convinced with the tone in Jill's voice, probed further.

"Really Dr.JP?"

Jill took the big step to unburden her tribulations on Cynthia.

At the end Dr. McAlister said, addressing Dr JP as Jill for a change "Jill, Dr. Higgin is right. I agree you need help, at least therapy if not medication. I can get you in to some EMDR treatment to start with."

Dr. McAlister was part of a program that treated people anonymously.

"Nobody at work needs to know."

"OK Cynthia." Jill finally gave in. "I expect to be back in a week."

"Do you think you need any medications in the mean time? Dr. Higgin or I can prescribe."

"No, No I will be fine." Jill had not told either of them that she, on her own, had started an antidepressant a few days ago which had not began to work yet. She was reluctant to take antipsychotic or alpha blockers for her dissociation, nightmares and flash backs.

The usually jovial crowd at the supper table kept silent tonight,

Even the drinking session was done in silence.

CHAPTER 17

DAY NINE

At the Mental health Center, the now familiar voice of JC greeted Jill.
The Hospital had discharged JC early this morning and he showed up for outpatient follow up with Dr. Perkins.
He did look much better than the first time she had met him though he continued to exhibit definite flavor of hypomania.

"Hey Doc how are you?" JC acknowledged his psychiatrist and her students, with a tip of his hat.
They lost their awe about of this bipolar person but perceived new admiration for treatment.

"Yes, the popular belief is that psychiatry is witch craft. On the contrary we do make people well or at least hold their illness in check."

"I prefer to keep people at a 6 rather than a 4. Even patients deserve a chance to enjoy life."

"I am going back to NOLA, Things, at least in the artsy sections like the French quarters, are looking up and some of the folks are returning. I can find a job and play music on the street."

"OK, make sure you take your medicine. I might come to NOLA next week before I leave LA and maybe I will run into you."

At one time the students did not believe they would get anything academic out of the current rotation but to their surprise the experience turned out to be educative and all three of them, Dr Perkins and Dr Hodges along with Mr. Paul Maslin taught them well. They hoped their replacements would be equally interested in teaching.

The tranquility of the uneventful morning exploded when Joanne phoned.

She sobbed again on the phone.
"What is it Joanne?" Jill noted a bit of impatience in her tone.

Tim was murdered last night."

The students discerned Dr. Perkins turn white.

"What happened?"

"I don't know much. The police told me they found Tim stabbed to death in one of the men's restrooms. His body has been taken away. "

Neither of them had anything to say.
They were at a loss to console each other.

Emotions of guilt and sadness tore into their hearts. They hung up without saying another word.

Davis, the police officer, walked in ready to be discharged. Brian had been skeptical about him all the time. He had a hard time hiding his disdain for wasting a perfectly good life. He, in some way, identified with Davis so the fact he had given up, had become an anathema to Brian.

He told the students." Let's go discharge him to the skid row. He will be back. They all play the revolving door game. They don't realize the Russian roulette they indulge in."

"Officer Davis, or should I say former Officer Davis, are you ready to go back to the Convention Center?"

Davis sensed the contempt in Dr Hodges voice. He had learned enough not to take the bait.

"Ah, Dr Hodges. Thank you for all your help. I am better now."

Brian turned his face towards the students and rolled his eyes. This too did not go unnoticed by Davis. But today, he was proud of himself.

"I hate to disappoint you." he laughed and added:"I am going back to NOLA."

"Really…" Brian stayed unconvinced.

"Yes, you might not think much of me, but you inspired me to go back to NOLA and return to the forces."

Brian was speechless when Davis shook his hands and bid goodbye.

Tammy as usual roamed the Dome looking for people in need.
She waved at the couple enjoying some coffee for a change. She politely declined the offer to join in. She smiled inside. What joy they had provided her. Much more exotic than the brew, it had been a different kind of threesome!

'Excuse me can you help me?"
Tammy turned to face an elderly woman.
She had fair skin but not like that of the Europeans. A cap covered her hair hiding it from Tammy.
She spoke in a clipped voice.

"How can I help you?"
"I am Vanessa"

"My grandson has been missing since we left Lake Charles right before Rita. I came to Lafayette on my way to Baton Rouge. I thought he went west towards Texas. I have not heard from him. I tried to talk with all kinds of officials here but none of them want to tell me or help me. I hope he is ok. He is a good boy. I have been bringing him up since

his father's murder, and his mother's incarceration. I am his only family. I know he can be a hot head. I hope he is not in any trouble."
She took out a faded picture of a young man.

"I am Tammy I am a social worker with mental health. I will make some enquires for you."

Tammy knew that in the aftermath of hurricanes Katrina and Rita, the U.S. Department of Justice has asked the National Center for Missing & Exploited Children (NCMEC) to staff a hotline to take reports of missing children, missing adults, and found children.

That would be the starting point.....

Paul checked on his vet friends.
They have been stable under the circumstances. The Vietnamese community of Lafayette had come looking for them. They wanted to take them both in to their folds.

"Well what do you think Mark?"
"Do you think you can handle living among the gooks?"
Paul didn't mince words. He wanted to be sure Mark would be stable.

"Yes I think I will be ok. I have no quarrel with these fine folks." he said putting his arm around the small Asian man.

Late that night they were drinking as usual but Tammy turned in early, returning to her room hoping, Denis, her new Cajun redneck, would call her. Brian usually does not join the four for the late drinks. Paul retired, claiming to be tired using his elderly status as a cover. In the last couple of days the other guest, the Gas man, as they jokingly called him, joined them for a drink or two but he always left early in the morning for work. He too called it a day to leave just Jill and Joanne sitting out in the patio.

The last few days have been traumatic for both of them. The two of them sat in the wicker chairs, deep in their own thoughts.

Joanne, during the last few days had been eyeing Jill in a different light. There has been some chemistry between them. Both were at loss to explain this electric charge. They didn't imagine it to be sexual in nature. Neither of them had experimented with other girls ever. Joanne, the older of the two, had an air of maturity about her that turned her seductive.

She stared at the garden in silence. Yesterday Joanne had helped Jill while she experienced an episode of flash back but the rawness of the experience weighed heavily on her mind. Joanne has assumed a protective role. A role she found exotic and maternal at the same time.

This was sad times for all of them. They had one bad news after another.

They took to heart the lost of the two strangers, the guardsman yesterday and Tim "the sexual change person" today.

Adding fuel to that fire,

Joanne had the troubling news from the home front and Jill continued her slippage into unknown depths with each passing day.

The nocturnal light on that full moon night gave the landscape a surreal yet soft gentle glow, as if it was all a part of a dream.

Jill had a sense of warmth all over.

"It must be the alcohol. I think I had a little too much to drink today." The Oban single malt bottle was empty. This was a taste she had inherited from Walter, who was a connoisseur of single malts.

"Jill, can I say something?" Joanne said softly.

Jill smiled at her older friend and replied "Of course Joanne, Anything for you Hun"

"I can't help but notice. I'm incredibly attracted to you." Those words popped out sensuously but neither felt awkward.

After a poignant silence, Jill asked.
"Do you want to kiss me Joanne?"

Jill barely heard herself over the drum beat of her own heart.

She brought her eyes to look into Joanne's, her cheeks flushing with excitement.

Joanne stared back at Jill, trying to figure out if she was serious or joking.
After a few long moments, her tongue ran across her lips, and she opened her mouth to speak.

"I'd love that" She replied.
"Then you can be my first" Jill enticed Joanne.

Joanne leaned closer to Jill. Her senses adored Jill's body heat and her sweet perfume. The Opium danced over her nostrils. Her breasts heaved against the red top she wore. Joanne slid her hand behind Jill's head and pulled her a little closer.

A soft Moan escaped Joanne. She locked her lips on to Jill's and kissed her hard. Her tongue slid past Jill's full ruby lips and began to explore the warm of her mouth. The kiss lasted a long time. An eternity or it seemed. The lips clung to each other's, sucking the sweet nectar.

This was their first kiss, a first with a woman for both.

They pulled back staring into the soul of each other through their eyes. Joanne gathered a fragile girl in her arms yearning to be loved.

Joanne's fingers slowly slide up Jill's side. It moved over her young perky breast. A tremble shook through Jill's insides and Joanne pulled her even closer. Joanne slowly began to unbutton the black blouse to reveal her pale skin and she kissed her neck and shoulders.

Jill remained silent, passive and yielding. Joanne reached back and unclasped Jill's bra.

"Shall we go inside?' Gently probed Joanne.
"Yes dear please.' Jill cooed inaudibly.
She was giddy with alcohol and desire.

Jill stood up but the room spun around her. She leaned on Joanne as she put an arm around Jill's slender waist. She guided the younger woman to their room.

A door from the patio led directly to their love nest.

In the room,

The fingers explored under the blouse and the bra to find the succulent breasts and the hard nipples which grew even firmer at the mere touch of Joanne's soft fingers.

"Mmm its feels good." beamed Jill enjoying the tactile sensation.

Jill kicked off her sandals and landed on her back on their king size bed.

Joanne kneeled before Jill and unzipped her jeans. Jill awake and sober yet drunk with lust raised her hip to let Joanne pull the tight jeans down to her ankles. She traced her fingers over her thighs. Jill gasped softly. Seeing Jill, naked and on her back in a vulnerable state, make Joanne horny. Jill dissociating from herself, enjoyed this admiration to the hilt. The top and the bra were long gone and in scintillating light, Jill looked like a princess.

Joanne kissed and rubbed Jill's flat stomach, guiding her palms down to her hips and she toyed with the waistband of the panties. She moved her probing fingers to her cotton panty covered Mon pubis.

Jill's lips quivered as she stared into Joanne's eyes and they were kissing again. Joanne felt the nipples hardening against the naked flesh. Leaning over her, she took Jill's breast into her mouth, sucking gently while she cuddled the other nipple between her thumb and finger. Her hand glided along the soft curvatures to the knee and back up again but between the thighs. Jill parted her thighs invitingly as Joanne caressed the silken inner thighs. Her exploring seductive fingers slowly moved up.

Joanne slide down and rested her face between Jill's thighs. Her fingers hooked the hem of the panties and pushed it aside so her lips could taste Jill for the first time. The probing tongue slid into warmth of Jill's inside. The flavorful juices drove her wild and took them both toward orgasm.

"God, yes hun!" Jill yelled in a raspy voice.

"Fuck me, Joanne, fuck me hard!"

Joanne licked her clit and began to glide a finger in and out of her pussy. She pumped in and out, slowly at first, but speeding up, in tune with the sounds of her lover's lustful moans. Jill's juices ran down Joanne's fingers as her arched her back offering herself to be taken and loved.

There were the sudden cascading orgasms lighting up the sky.

Later, Jill returned the favor of loving her soul mate.

Long after, after hours of joyous and erotic love making, they lay there for a long time, just cuddling each other, naked, exhausted, and soaking in the tremendous gratification.

CHAPTER 18

DAY TEN

They were in the eye of the storm. Everything around them turned calm and quiet while the world churned.

Wilma swayed away from them in a heartening wave of winds.

In the Dome, most of their wards reached relative stability. The deaths of the two seem far beyond the glossy horizon.

For Jill and Joanne, the episode of last night seemed nothing but a fuzzy dream.

A different journey and destination awaited them today.

Andrea and Jim announced the arrival of the successor group at Lake Charles. The plans comprised of a trip towards west and bring the newbie's up to speed.

Before they reached Lake Charles, a circular path through the Creole natural trail, one of the first national scenic byways, awaited them. Many of the towns along this 180 mile route had been hit by Rita. Their mission included checks on the shelters en route to assess the acute needs so the arriving group could follow through.

The travel to the west, to meet up with the second bunch, became another eye opener for all. Hurricane Rita had caused catastrophic damage in southwestern Louisiana. The winds had spared the city of Lafayette per se but they had a glimpse of the furry on their maiden travel to the Vermillion bay and Cypermort point.

On Interstate 10 they passed Crawley.
Joanne reminisced her stay. Images of Tim flooded her mind and she had to make a tremendous effort to hold back her tears. Loss of Tim's life had sprayed blood of guilt over her heart. It would take ages to live that down.

Last week they had gone to Crawley during the international Rice festival. They had a wonderful experience that night except for Brian and Tammy. They missed the greater part of the festivities because Brian, driving with Tammy, took a wrong turn earlier in their dash to the show. They failed to realize their folly and almost ended up in Baton Rouge.

After they crossed Crawley, they passed many tent cities harboring the displaced people.
Just before they reached the city of Lake Charles, they turned off I 10 to state route 397 and drove towards 14 and on to scenic 27.

Scenic is a relative term. Route 27 definitely was a glorious trail before the hurricane, but now, all that remained was an utterly devastated country side mile after mile.

In the costal parish of Cameron, the towns of Creole, Holly Beach, Hackberry, Grand Chenier and downtown Cameron, nearly 95 percent, roughly 5,000 homes suffered severely damage or worse got destroyed.

All along, they witnessed destruction on either side of the of the west Creole highway. They passed a church without a roof with the icons laid bare on murky lawns in the rubble. They drove through the Cameron parries national wide life reserve. An eerie silence greeted them. Significant by their absence, the sound of the birds chirping, colored the landscape. They turned west ward before Oak grove. They skipped grand Chenier on Oak grove highway. They followed 27 and 82 running together until they came to Downtown Cameron.

The municipal building stood alone among the ruins left untouched as it sat on higher ground.

Everything else was disseminated.

Signs of FEMA sprouted everywhere, side by side with less advertized yet equally conspicuous Private contractors in huge buses. These high tech buses would make any Si Fi movie blush with envy. They reminded Jill of the UN black helicopters, the conspiracy theorists whispered in fringe chat rooms. They ran into the mercenaries along the desolate gulf beech highway connecting Cameron to Port Arthur, Texas. They wondered what the Para military protected other than wild alligators.

They eyed the off shore oil rigs' out in the ocean, a force de tat.

Cameron boasted of reliance. They repeatedly get wiped out by the hurricanes. The natives of the Cameron parish rebuild their city again and again.

Some voluntary group from a church in Texas fed the citizens.

FEMA made signs for people's houses due to absence of road and land signs.
They realized that the city remained in acute phase and the next group would have more work to do.

They moved on. Around the junction where 82 and 27 split, they came upon Holly Beech, a resort town called the Rivera of Louisiana. This beach town's image got etched in their psyche as the nature's calling card of divine intervention. Roads and sand dunes greeted them. The whole city did not have a single structure. The storm surge of 12 feet had completely wiped out the town.

As they stood on the desolate beach, the lone testimonial was an American Flag that someone had proudly placed after the hurricane.

They reached Johnson bayou where Rita had made first land fall. Complete desolation accosted them. On their way back, they stumbled upon those shady big buses again. They wondered if they had aroused the interest of independent contractors.

They also witnessed rangers wrestling with alligators and putting them in the pickup. Devoid of any native population to speak of along the Gulf beech highway, the alligators ruled the road and roamed free.

Back on 27 they turned north passing Mud Lake and West cove all desolate and barren. and then they reached Hackberry, LA, another hard hit town.

A big hall functioned as a place for folks to go for food, clothes, dry goods, medicine .At this resource bank of sorts; they made contact with an advance party from Lake Charles.
The solidarity among the natives impressed the outsiders. The support these people provided for each other would prevent PTSD.

Indeed it takes a village to prevent PTSD!

They stopped for Gas at Carlyss along the 27 and realized they had seen pictures of this station.

Well it was way under water then... The attendant showed them a picture of gushing waters.

This ravenously hungry bunch trooped into the eatery attached to the gas station.
They were treated to a foodie crash course in the ultimate Cajun cuisine.

The treat in store for them included Boudin, a pork casing filled with pork rice dressing (includes liver and heart meats) and or sea food. They ate it with cracklins (pig skin fried) and dressing. The outside world still fancy the jambalaya, gumbo and the dirty rice but boudin is fast growing in popularity.

Tammy, a foodie among the five had on occasion made dishes for all of them in Mary's house. She watched the woman prepare the food. She realized they used the mixture of the aromatic vegetables. The holy trinity of bell pepper (poivron) onion and celery quite similar to the French mire poix (onion/celery and carrot). The Cajuns also added parsley, bay leaf, scallions and cayenne pepper. She made a light roux with flour and bacon fat. She kept the sauce light as she makes a sea food gumbo. Tammy had tasted the generic gumbo before which had always used the dark roux with the nutty flavor favored by the gamey gumbo.

The meal came with boudin blanc, one devoid of blood, and a sea food gumbo with shrimp, fish and crawfish meat.

They had a side of maque choux, braised vegetable mix of corn, bell pepper, celery, onions, tomatoes and garlic.

Couche Couche, a Cajun corn mush also adorned the platter.

With gas in the tank and full bellies, thcy reached Lake Charles completing a circle. The experience stacked tremendous understanding of the suffering many folks had endured. They had treated similar people at Lafayette.

In downtown Lake Charles, downed trees lay along the streets. These huge trees had lined the roads for hundreds of years. They noted houses with the trendy blue tarp covering the roof blown away in the 150 mph winds,

They met rest of the Lake Charles team at the hospital. Andrew, Neil and Dawn had accompanied them back after the visit to the relief center at Hackberry.

This team led by a psychiatrist from Boston included Nancy and Cathy.

Dr Golden had been working at Mass General and decided to give up some time for a good cause.

They spend a few hours seeing the patients at the primary shelter.
Jill led the way being the experienced one. The population and procedures remained the same.

Dr Golden was very impressed by the leadership of Jill.

When evening dawned on them, they said goodbyes and went on to their roosting nests.

The drive back to Lafayette was somber. The trip had been a monotonous drain on the mind and soul.

After supper they retired to bed early san their usual drinking session

Jill and Joanne lay awake in bed in silence.

CHAPTER 19

DAY ELEVEN

Jill woke up in Joanne's arms.
She had rolled over during the sleep. She sat up and startled Joanne.

"Is everything ok? Are you upset over what happened between us the other night? I am sorry if you were hurt?"

"No worries, I don't have any regrets. Qui sera sera. We enjoyed the fuck let's wait for the future to unfold." Joanne searched Jill's face for answers startled by the callousness in Jill's voice.

They both enjoyed the tender and romantic love making but neither, without any past experiences to bank on, fully fathomed the meaning.

Jill continued her downward spiral. She had dissociations, panic attacks and even a psychotic loss of touch with reality.

"I can't grasp who I am anymore; or my feelings towards others."
"My sexuality has transgressed to areas where I had never gone before."

She could not make sense of her the new found personality. She regressed into depths unknown.

Andrea informed Jill to expect a new group who will be their replacement.

The leader of the group, Andrea said, was a nurse practitioner. She has a Ph.D." Her name is Jan. I hope the older therapists in the group would be ok with their younger captain."
"I got baptized by fire."She will come on top too. "

JC left for NOLA. He had a month's supply of his medications. His blood levels checked yesterday, proved good.
She did didactics teaching for a change. It was never her forte but she had some time before she headed to the Dome. They talked about psychiatry and covered many topics.

Today was Friday, the last day they would spend with Dr Perkins and her group.
They expected new educators when they come back from the weekend on Monday.
Goodbyes were in order.

The students showed their appreciation by giving Dr Perkins a copy of The Cajun Blood CD by Jo-El Sonnier. They knew she was fond of Cajun music.

Davis went back. He had left a small memento for Brian to show his appreciation too.

Paul and Jill had lunch together again.
"You are moody Jill."
"Oh I am sorry." Paul noticed a vacant reflection on her face.
"What is wrong Jill? Tell me, I can be of some help."

"Thanks Paul, I am Ok. I have many things on my mind."
"Well if you need me you know where to find me." Paul though not happy with Jill's suffering, respected her privacy.

"By the way, what's up with you and Joanne? You two behave like quarreling lovers." He laughed.
"Oh shut up Paul."

Paul had no clue to the recent interlude, but he sensed tension between them in the last couple days.

She walked back to the dome.

Jim appeared less anxious. He confided that he had taken her advice and had started seeing the therapist and the psychiatrist at the base.

As she went past him, he cracked off a smart salute and she returned one. Her eyes gazed on the empty spot where Bill used to stand guard....

He was a dark quiet man; Jill spotted him sitting by himself in an empty hallway, his back to the wall.
He stared past the parking lots and the wide open spaces.

What got Jill's attention was the vacant look on his face she had been seeing in the mirror, in the last few months.

"Hello" she said very gently.
In spite of her gentleness he jumped and got into a crouching position. He appeared like a panther ready to pounce at the first sign of danger.

When he noted Jill, he sort of relaxed.

"I am sorry I startled you."

"I am sorry I jumped at you."

"You are sad."

"Yes I am."

She went on to take a history. He remained very cryptic in his answers but to Jill's trained ear he did have enough signs of depression though he completely denied any symptom of PTSD or anxiety.

He agreed to try some medication and she decided to start him on Remeron for depression. She explained the side effects to him. He listened carefully and patiently.
At the end he lifted his tee shirt.

"Will the medication hurt this?"He pointed to his muscular chest.

Mesmerized by large scars just over and around his left nipple, she remained speechless, staring at his battle scared chest wall.

"Are they stab wounds? She peered in to his cool eyes wondering who he might be.
Before she could ask, he said softly "Yes ma'am they are knife wounds. I have been stabbed many times."

Jill took out the pills, a 2 weeks supply, but from corner of her eye she noted a tear drop roll down his eyes…

She gave him the medication but did not say good bye or get up to move on as she would normally do.

They both sat there in silence.
Just the two of them.
She heard their heart beats.
He kept his head down.
His breathed deep and then he started to cry….

Jill did not say a word but gently placed her hand on his…
Waiting for him to take the lead.
Waiting for the catharsis...

She became privy to one of the most incredulous stories.
He was at the OPP when the storm hit.

"Orleans Parish Prison (OPP) is actually a county jail, a temporary detention facility. It is one of the largest "jails "in the country. At any given time, there would be 7,500 to 8,000 prisoners and just before the storm another 2000 inmates evacuated to OPP."

"The inmates are a mixed crowd. Some of them serving misdemeanor sentences while others are parole violators but majority are pretrial detainees. Some are for not paying a fine, jay walking public intoxication, begging or homeless and vagabonds.
They are violent inmates, adult and juvenile.
They also had federal prisoners.'

He continued in a monotone.

"The Templeman III building had two levels of cells." The upper level remained open because of the overcrowding. While others were locked in the cells down stairs"

"There was no evacuation plans before the hurricane. It appeared as if the prisoners and guards alike were left there. It is possible the sheriff thought they would be ok there, the storm would pass and life would go on as normal on Tuesday.
The mandatory evacuation spanned the city except for the thousands of prisoners and their guards. 'We will leave them in the jail where they belong the sheriff had said. 200 animals in the shelter across town got evacuated instead."

"As the hurricane came closer, the guards became more aware of their plight and fled, leaving the prisoners locked up inside the walls of the facility."

"We lost power"

"As the floodwaters rose after the storm had passed on Monday, there was no food or water for days. The power had been off since Monday. Deputies left behind, had brought in their families for safety."

The first floor of Templeman 111 was chest high under water. The central lock up, a single story building was completely under water."

"There was total chaos"
"People screamed for help"
"People were standing in toxic water and dead bodies and rats floated by."
"Stories floated about inmates and staff being killed."

"Through the night I heard Cries of death ethos, and moans of people drowning."
"Groans of people being gnawed by rats."
"I drank water that had feces floating in it"
"I ate rotten food and much more to survive"

"I finally broke out. I escaped, swimming through the water, during the night. "
"I dare not do it in day light because the deputy snipers picked people off as they tried to get off by jumping into water. They must have felt like fish in a barrel. Some of them had no crime against their names other than being homeless and seeking food because they were hungry."

Now…

"At night, I still hear them cry."
"I hear them dying."
"I hear the sound of the gushing water."
"I sense the gnawing rats on my body, thousands of them crawling on my skin, looking for a juicy bite of my flesh."
"Yes here I am. I can never go back to the prison.
"I rather die"

There was more silence.

Then he got up thanked Jill.

"Ma'am not many people have shown me any kindness in my life. I will always remember you."
He gave her hand a gentle squeeze and stood up towering over her.
He lowered his head and planted a kiss on her forehead, turned and walked away.

Jill never saw him again.

Jill stared past the gates long after he had left.

In the dancing flames of the dusk she wondered who he was.
A homeless man; a returning soldier; a jay walker, a white collar federal prisoner; a man who forgot to pay his fine or traffic ticket: a rapist or maybe a mass murderer?

She would never know!

Brian met Mary and Patches again. He looked out for them. He had grown fond of them. She reminded him of his grand ma.

"I listened to you. I have not been feeding Patches." Brian noticed that she had washed the chocolate stain away.

"Sit down son. I have been thinking. What will happen to Patches when I die, I had thought about having him buried with me but that would be cruel to him?"

"I will take care of Patches." He promised her.

"You are a good boy." She seems so relived....

Joanne learned more gruesome details of Tim's death.
" They sodomized him many times with a flash light before they cut his throat. Joanne remembered the flash light Tim had carried with him."
"More than one person brutalized him according to the police."

"It was a hate crime towards an innocent person."

" Words scrawled across the wall of the restroom reverberated with hate and fear."

" GOD HATES AND PUNISH THE WEIRDOS AND FAGGOTS. "

Tanya finally caught up with Brian
"Have you been avoiding me Dr Hodges?"
Brian did not know what to say.
Tammy had not told him about her recent encounter. She wanted him to learn the true side of Tanya on his own.
"I am sorry for being so rude that day."
"No hard feelings?" She held out her hand.
Brian took her hand and shook it.
He did not utter a single word.
He turned and walked away still in shock.

He turned his head after few minutes and found joy in the fact that she kept looking at him. As their eyes met, they smiled at each other. Without hesitation Brian walked back towards her.......

The couple had news for Tammy. They got a FEMA trailer in Lake Charles and they will be moving back. They thanked Tammy for her support. She shyly stated "I did not do much for you."
"Oh no, you did dear, you respected us."

As the two middle aged love birds walked away, hand in hand, Tammy continued to admire them from far with a smile on her face.

"I wonder what they would say about our virtual 3some!"

Brian spent an hour with Mindy. Stable for the present, she had refrained from further cutting. She did not make any more threats of killing herself or burning the place down and she was even in good terms with the Red Cross. She had not been on any medications.
He now had another hard task ahead of him.
He has to terminate with her which would be another crisis in Mindy's life. He wondered if someone in the community could do some work with her or one in the new team.

Sociopath Ken was still in jail, The Red Cross informed Brian. He also noticed melting ice in their frigid ways towards him.

Paul checked on his Vet twins before they left for Little Vietnam.

Paul ran into Jules the hit man, a restless soul. He continued to suffer the pain of his past crimes. "You should seek a priest" Paul told him He might find solace in religion.

Vanessa searched for Tammy.
"I don't have any more information but I will keep looking."
Tammy did not have the heart to embrace the pain on her face.

She knew they had a broken criminal justice system.

They had been aware of the horror stories of OPP being a black hole. And today Jill had just told them her strange encounter. Tammy wondered where Vanessa's grandson was.

Joanne came across her first patient again

The same big man with beady eyes visibly agitated. Joanne knew that look. She had seen one too many of those in the detox wards back home.

She had seen him in similar state days ago.

The usual symptoms remained.

"Sweating"
"Dilated pupils and tearing eyes"
"The runs and abdominal cramps."
He was yawning too.

He demanded she give him something for his heroin withdrawal.

Oxycontin? Vicodin? Seroquel? Not even vistoril?
"No sir, not even methadone or suboxone" Joanne said and made her exit again.

Jenna met Tammy with another man. She quickly realized that he was a major.

"This is major Rifkin. He is from JAG. He is going to help me file charges. I am going to take control of my life. I am no longer the victim. Thank you for all your help."

Joanne stopped by Mike the homeless man. She had hoped good things for him but was disappointed.
"I am going to NOLA" and he walked away. She had the feeling that he might remain homeless for a while.

They were all leaving the dome together, for a change. They got the message John Doe indeed had a UTI. He also was low in B12 and thyroid. They decided to keep him at the hospital for couple of days before they sent him to the Nursing home. He remained demented and would progressively get worse. At least he would be cared for until someone shows up for him.

They were buoyant than usual as things seemed to look up for most of the people they came into contact.

Jill was not sure if they could say the same for the members of the team.

.
She did talk to Walter and Cynthia before she went to sleep.

She completely avoided the group activity.

She had a nightmare again.

Gruesome as it sounds; Jill in some ways, got used to them by now, at least the part in the London tube.

But tonight the drama took a turn for the worse.

The dream got more complex. She had moved from England to the Middle East. Dressed in army uniform, she had lined up dozens of Cajun women and children and began shooting them.

She stripped each of them naked. made them lie on their belly and with the barrel of the m16, sodomized each one of them.

She shrieked with joy of maddening laughter that rose and drowned the wrenched cry of the tortured souls.
Then she blasted rounds into the belly as the human flesh splattered her face and she, drenched in excreta and blood continued to laugh.

She had the feeling of choking and drowning. She heard her own raspy breathing.

Thrashing and fighting the unknown demons, she woke up from yet another nightmare.

The two of them, Jill and Joanne kept Virgil for the rest of the night.

CHAPTER 20

DAY TWELVE

The dawn ushered in the changing of the Guards.
The new group landed last night. There will be some days of overlap which would make the transition seamless as possible. Jill and her crew got ready to meet with them.

"So the leader is a nurse practitioner" Brian stated matter of fact at the breakfast table.

"Brian is that a question or a statement?" bristled Jill.

They had been too engrossed in the events of the week, they had forgotten their rivalry.

Days ago this interaction would have taken a variant path.

Without waiting for his reply Jill ploughed on." I know it's not a genuine question but rather a rhetorical one. If you are making a statement on your views about female

hegemony, I have already proven to you my superior leadership capabilities." Brian's eyes widened hearing her verbal challenge.
This was an aspect of Jill's character they had not witnessed. She was assertive but exuded diplomacy. Today she sounded short tempered and mean.

Jill continued her rant.

"You are opinionated, sexist and a racist. You are an Asshole Brian."

Mary and John sensed an uneasy atmosphere.

Everyone had noticed positive changes in Brian. Though core values would still harbor old and negative feelings, he opened up to others. They began to sense warmth under the cold robotic Brian and started to appreciate him.

He loosened up too and validated by saying.

"Hey, who says I am a racist? I am not a WASP but just a mutt, a proud one. I learned, not too many days ago, that I am a bastard born out of wedlock to my mother and my real father, a Lebanese!"

A wave of relief flowed down his body.

Everyone was stunned, not by the substance of his revelation, but the way he had progressed miles from his prudish stance, less than 2 weeks ago.

"And I have a date with Tanya." He made his crowning statement with a twinkle in his eyes.

"No Kidding, Way to go Brian", Tammy high fived Brian. Tammy, amused at the turn of events, stamped her seal of approval. "She is hot I am telling you,"

"Jill, I learned a significant amount about myself during this time. I also gained a lot from you. This experience made me a better man; I want to thank you and every one of you."

Jill, lost in her own crumbling world, stayed reticent.

Andrea breezed in with the new contingent. They lodged at the Beaux Bridge B & B last night and would continue to do so until Jill's team finished their tour of duty. They had dropped in on their way to the Center. They wore similar SAMHSA tee shirts and appeared enthusiastic. The presence of strangers eased the tension in the room.

An all female group, lead by Jan came in and Jan shook hands with Jill.

"Dr Perkins, I heard so many good things about you. I am disappointed I would not work with you. Dr Hesston from SAMSA and the leadership are mighty impressed. Those are large shoes to fill." Jan smiled.

"You guys will move in here a few days after they leave." said Andréa.

"Mary and John are the best." quipped Joanne. She had been at both the places, and even though she greatly appreciated the other owners, Mary and John made up a unique couple and an institution.

"Let's go to the Center. Jan's team can shadow Jill's for the day.

Monty, Debbie, Rose Marie, Susan and Jen.

.

After formal introductions, they shared some intriguing stories to prepare the Newbie's for the grinding task ahead.

"Most of our patients are stable or moved out.

"A couple of them moved out of this world altogether."

This stunned the fervent crew and Paul enlightened them.

"Who opt to stay at the Center this morning?"Jill enquired. "There is some heavy lifting to be done here. Besides you also do some teaching to the medical students.

"I will do that." Jan stated, erasing any challenges to her position. Jill concluded the leadership was in sound hands.

They continued their efforts in the inpatient unit until lunch time. Jan lingered in the background as an observer fascinated by the work of Paul and Jill.

Brian, Tammy and Joanne took the other four to the Dome and the convention center.

Brian assumed the de facto leadership of the group in Jill's absence. Neither Joanne nor Tammy object to this, they had grown fond of the ex socially inept Brian.

Tanya had joined the VOA as a volunteer.
"The new uniform looks nice on you Tanya" said Brian.
"Wow who are all the pretty ladies with you? You are moving up in the world Dr. Hodges."
"You should have seen these two on the first day we met Tanya." laughed Tammy.
"They were ready to tear each other apart."

"We were just a couple of ignorant racist rednecks weren't we Tanya?" Brian chided.
"Yes, fear and prejudice are great driving forces…."

"Hey drop the charade Tanya. Brian here has the hots for you. What a change of events. Thank God she is not our patient."

Tammy and Joanne had warm regards for the two of them.

Brian and Tanya maintained a tacit silence.

Tammy walked tepidly to the area once occupied by her exotic and erotic couple. Any signs this eight feet by six feet piece of universe, belonged to the illustrious two, had vanished from the face of the earth. This oyster had new tenants. The group stopped by their palatial abode to chat with them.

As the gang moved on, Tammy looked back with a sigh.

Life goes on…

"Joanne and Tammy, will you continue the tour with the new folks while I take Rose Marie to visit my ward?"
"Oh, you are dumping your borderline on poor Rose Marie. Sure Brian, and be careful of his ways RoseMarie."

On their way Rose Marie had talked about working with BPD using DBT. Brian realized the new therapist for Mindy would be this wonderful woman.

Mindy was upset with Brian. The talk of his departure did not sit well with her.
She had cut her forearm night before.
The Red Cross had followed his advice at last.
The clinic stitched her up, bandaged her, and kept Mindy to have therapy with Brain this morning.

Brian beamed at his astute selection.

Mindy had placed Rose Marie on the pedestal already.

He knew she was in good hands in her world of absolute black and white.

"Ken is still in jail."

"We had a hard time convincing the official what we do in mental health. They used to send us anti socials while they dispatched sick people to the jail but in the end they wised up. I don't think you would have any trouble at all." Brain gave Rose Marie a synopsis of their past interaction with the officials.

The Red Cross had a surprise for Brian. They informed him of an important inheritance that he had been given this morning.

"Who would be sending me anything at all?

It was Patches.

Mary had passed away peacefully in her sleep at night, but not before sharing with one of the staff that if she died, they had to give her dog to that young man who had come to see her, the last couple of days.
She was at peace with herself and the world with the knowledge, her dog Patches ,was safe and would be well taken care of!

Tammy cringed at Vanessa's voice
She gave her apologies and introduced the new members.
"Ms: Vanessa these people will be taking over from me.
They will continue to look for your grandson."

"Well we cannot win all the battles can we?"

Jennifer continued to do good... "That is your eating disorder patient but she is stable, at least for the time being."

She also shared the story of the discrimination; she had faced at the clinic, which astonished the new members.

"Be wary of this big man; he will hit you up for narcotics." Joanne was updating them about the drug addict.

"And there is a young man named Mike. He is a sad story." He is a handsome young man who is homeless. Yesterday he had told us of his trip to NOLA, but who knows, he might show up here again. There is not much we can do for him. Maybe help him with some antidepressant…"

They picked up new patients as the day went on replacing the old and the dead ones. The strain of misery, mayhem, and death had left new wrinkles of sorrow on their faces in such a short time. Their lives would never be the same again.

The three of them ate lunch together.
Jill had recovered somewhat after this morning's tirade.

"What was that all about Dr Perkins?" enquired Paul as they sat eating lunch. They introduced Jan to the pleasures of Cajun cuisine.

"What do you think? He had to be put in his place." snapped Jill but with less ferocity than in the morning. Paul did not want to take it any further especially in Jan's presence. He let it slide and they moved on to neutral topics of food and state of mental health in the country.

They left for dome after lunch.

"Paul ca you drive Jan to the Dome and show her around? I will join you two later; I have to make a couple of calls to Pittsburgh before returning to work."

"Sure Dr. Perkins." Paul took off with Jan.

Jill decided to disclose everything to Dr. Higgin or Dr. McAlister.
She, for the first time, became concerned about the path her life was leading her.

She called but voice mails greeted her on both their phones. "Well I have to wait." Jill acknowledged her loss of control.

As she walked alone into the Dome, for one last time, Jill remembered her first visit here. The panic attack was clearly etched in her memory.
An uneasy aura came over her as this uneasiness had become her companion.

“Mental health yeah?”
“We need a lot of that around here starting with me.”
She had heard those words before. They came from Bill.

"But Bill is dead isn't he? "

"Is he beckoning her?"

She kept moving.

As she turned the corner she was engulfed by a flood of milling population.
Same faces she met two weeks ago. Familiar yet strange.
They waved and smiled at her as if they knew who she was but she did not recognize any.

She appeared to be nauseous and queasy in her stomach.

She headed further through the double doors and she stood at the threshold of the dome.

A stream of sweat flowed down the side of her face along her sharp cheek.

Her heart began to pound.
The breath grew dyspneic. She gasped for air; hungry to fill her oxygen starved lungs.
Her hands were tremulous and her legs seemed made of jelly.
She was light headed and dizzy.

“Oh my God it's happening again."

She was not sure if she was back in her nightmare. The one she had last night.
Is this Lafayette or Iraq? Are the people around her Iraqi or Americans?

"Bill Bill please doesn't kill me".

"Isn't that Bills' wife pleading with him not to shot her?"

Her eyes filled with tears and gun smoke and she could not make out if it was Bill's wife or the electrician's. They looked the same .They both grew wings and flew away from her like angels.

A crowd of people, police men wearing LA state uniform, electrician, Jim in National Guard uniform and a bunch of Middle Eastern men in their flowing gowns and checkered turbans all stomped her.

She eyed Brian, dressed like the Lawrence of Arabia but naked below the waist trying to stop them.

“I am having a heart attack.”

Jill experienced excruciating pain over the sternum.

The boots pounded on her chest.

“I am dying,”

The dreaded sensation reached a crescendo.
“I have to get away to safety or I would die here.”

She ran back through the double doors out into the open. "Escape, escape, I must escape....."

The walls of the building began to close around her and sweaty bodies pressed against her.
She lost touch with reality. And what was reality anyway?

She eyed herself now.
She noticed Mike in a white robe waving and beckoning her, and Bill in starched uniform with his shinny medals of war.

The sound of the subway interspaced the explosions of the IED hammering in her ears white the rattle of gun fire shattered Mikes and Bills head.

She crouched in a corner doubled up and vulnerable like a little girl.

She waited to die! Again.

"Dr Perkins are you ok?" She opened her eyes and saw Jim, the national guardsman.

They both instantly appreciated what she had just experienced.

"I get them too" he said in his usual soft voice. "They are better now thanks to you, Doctor. I am in treatment and taking medications. Maybe you should seek help too."

He pleaded with the doctor, who had saved his life.

Paul caught up with Jill and noted the pale reflection that he had seen before. He exchanged silent looks but did not talk about it in Jan's presence.

"I am sorry it took me longer than I thought. I still have not got hold of them."
"Paul, please continue to show Jan around. I have a few more errands."
Without waiting for a reply she started to walk away.

"Oh, introduce, Jan to the red Cross and the VOA and of course the national guard." She delegated her work to Paul. Paul knew something was wrong. Paul would have intervened if it wasn't for Jan's presence.

Joanne had earlier spoken to him in private about the nightmare last night.
They were worried for their friend.....

Jill walked towards the Convention Center. She never liked the Center. She found it dark and foreboding. Today, she for some reason, perceived a magnetic pull to it. They had found Tim in one of those rest rooms.

She sat on the floor of the restroom, crying. She could hear the cries of Tim, begging for mercy.

Andrea and Jim invited them to their home hosting a party in their honor.
Jim, an excellent cook treated them to a great feast of Cajun dinning.

"He makes the best gumbo in the world."Piped Andréa as she watched folks gather round the pot Jim made his gumbo.

He lectured to the folks like a gastronomy professor.

"The word gumbo comes from the African word for okra, kigombo; in the classical gumbo we need okra. It is used as the thickener. In the later years roux and file replaced okra."
"Roux is basically a mixture of flour and butter (or lard); while file is a powdered form of dried sassafras leaves. We make chicken and andoullie sausage or sea food gumbo."
"Unlike the Creole we do not put tomatoes in it"
He added his secret ingredients.

The feast included Boudin blanc pork, craw fish pie, and stuffed crab for appetizers. Jambalaya, shrimp etouffee and the gumbo as main dishes and for desert they had bread pudding with whiskey sauce.

Though many among them had dined at famous places like the blue dog café, Prejeans and Johnson's Boucaniere, Jim's and Andrea's dinner seemed to be the best.

They had dined on the best food that Acadiana had to offer. The only thing they had not tasted was a Turducken.
"What is it?"
"It is a three deboned bird roast. Chicken in duck and those two baked inside a deboned turkey. The spaces
usually stuffed with corn and sausages and other meats."
"The American Turducken, originated at the Hebert's Specialty Meats" in Maurice, Vermillion parish. The store is not too far from here. I think we drove in front of it the first time we drove around." Andrea explained.

In a pensive mood Jim shared a beer and moment of serenity with Jill.
"Jill we were so lucky to have you here. If you consider moving south we would have a job for you and you can make a home with us."
He sounded paternal.
Emotions swelled up in Jill and all she could say was a meek "thank you Jim."

Later, as a group, they talked about the bus trip to NOLA.

Initially Jill had her reservations but they had promised armed guards in each bus. She still had her doubts though she had agreed.
They discussed and though with ambiguity, they did want to make that journey. What was a trip to LA without one to NOLA?

Did their ego and fantasies get better of their rational intellectual thinking?

Well Dr Perkins had been having difficulty with reality testing anyways!

CHAPTER 21

DAY THIRTEEN

NOLA- A Tale of Two Cities

It was ravaged by a disaster which not only caused human and property damage but also exposed the American culture in many areas.

This was not a natural disaster. The direct effect of Hurricane Katrina was not any more than the usual damage the city endures annually during the hurricane season. This was a manmade disaster.

On August 28, the National Weather Service (NWS) field office in New Orleans issued a bulletin predicting catastrophic damage to New Orleans and the surrounding region.

"The partial destruction of half of the well-constructed houses in the city, severe damage to most industrial buildings, rendering them inoperable, the "total destruction" of all wood-framed low-rise apartment buildings, all windows blowing out in high-rise office buildings, and the creation of a huge debris field of trees, telephone poles, cars, and collapsed buildings. Lack of clean water predicted to "make human suffering incredible by modern standards." They predicted the standing water caused by the storm surge would render most of the city uninhabitable for weeks and the destruction of oil and petrochemical refineries in the surrounding area will spill waste into the flooding. The resulting mess would coat every surface, converting the city into a toxic marsh until water could be drained. Some experts said it could take six months or longer to pump all the water out of the city. "

In a live news conference, Mayor Nagin predicted, "the storm surge most likely will topple our levee system", President Bush made a televised appeal for residents to heed the evacuation orders, warning, "We cannot stress enough the danger this hurricane poses to Gulf Coast communities."

Although Mayor ordered a mandatory evacuation of the city, tens of thousands of citizens refused to leave, with numerous explanations that included a belief that they would ride out the storm, lack of financial resources or access to transportation, or a sense of obligation to protect their property.

A "refuge of last resort" was designated at the Louisiana Superdome. Beginning at noon on August 28 city buses were redeployed to shuttle local residents from pickup points throughout the city to the "shelters of last resort." The Superdome had been used as a shelter in the past.

It was estimated approximately one million people had fled the city and its surrounding area but over 100,000 people remained in the city, with 20,000 taking shelter at the Louisiana Superdome, along with 300 National Guard troops

Katrina passed South-east of New Orleans on the morning of August 29, 2005, winds were in the Category 3 strength. The city per se avoided significant damage from the hurricane, even prompting headlines proclaiming

"NOLA dodges Katrina."

But soon after the storm passed, In the City of New Orleans, the storm surge caused so many breaches in canal levees including the 17th Street Canal levee, the Industrial Canal levee, and the London Avenue Canal floodwall, and precipitated the worst engineering disaster in the history of the United States.

By 11:00 pm on August 29, there were reports of bodies floating on the water in the eastern parts of the city. There was no clean water or electricity in the city, and some hotels and hospitals reported diesel fuel shortages.

The extensive flooding stranded many residents, who remained stranded for many days after the Hurricane had passed. Some were trapped inside attics, unable to escape. Many others chopped their way onto their roofs with hatchets and sledge hammers. These stranded survivors were on the houses tops as they sought dry ground. Coordination of rescue efforts on August 29 and August 30 were made difficult by disruption of the communications infrastructure .Most of the major roads traveling into and out of the city were damaged. The only route out of the city was west on the Crescent City Connection as the I-10 Twin Span Bridge traveling east towards Slidell, had collapsed eliciting the infamous picture of the bridge to nowhere.

The Superdome sustained significant damage, including two sections of the roof that were compromised.

On August 30; Louisiana governor Kathleen Blanco ordered the complete evacuation of the remaining people.

By August 31, 80% of New Orleans was flooded, with some parts under 15 feet of water.

There were many deaths, mainly from drowning and unprecedented property loss.

The damage and reactions were of near apocalyptical in intensity.

In the aftermath of Hurricane Katrina, looting, violence and other criminal activity became serious problems. Several news sources reported instances of fighting, drug use, theft, rape, and murder in the Superdome and other refuge centers. Some initial reports of mass chaos, particularly in stories about the Superdome, were later found to be exaggerated or just unfounded rumors.

Weeks after this calamity, Jill and her crew planned the trip to the city on the penultimate day of their sojourn in LA.

They were excited.

They had seen media reports and had followed the raging national discourse on it. They had privy to some harrowing stories from the people who had lived through the hurricane and had migrated to Lafayette.

.

But today they set out to gather firsthand experience of the city.

This would make up for some of the letdown they experienced when ordered to go to Lafayette instead of the eye of the disaster storm. They were surprised by the intensity of their experience at a place, hours from the city, but this trip construed a pilgrimage they all wanted to make.
This made them gloss over the potential pit falls.

CHAPTER 22

DAY THIRTEEN

A TRIP TO ETERNITY

The buses lined up like decorated elephants in an Indian Temple festival.

There were five buses.

The adventure to ferry the expatriates from New Orleans, back to their homeland for one last fleeting look-in boasted of a grand gesture on surface but a class if not ethnic cleansing, American style in reality.

The rubble of houses demolished by the winds and the water, and those partially ravished by the furry of nature would all be razed to ground by the machines of reconstruction.

Powerful entities vied for opportunistic land grab and gentrification under the guise of the new paradigm for rebirth.

The struggle, often paraded as a racial confrontation, indeed represented a subterranean class conflict. They did not want the poor to return to the city. One of the nefarious plans to achieve this aspiration depended on destroying the properties untouched by the hurricane.

The trip functioned as pilgrimage for the residents, not to rebuild but to walk away from their communities, to take one last glance at their homes, gather any valuables, and melt way into the wood work of the society.

Jill had her doubts when this trip incubated in its rudimentary planning stage. She had expressed strong reservations claiming it would be grandiosely generous to even call this a half baked plan.
Her rationalization pointed out the dangerousness of the poorly concocted plan that consisted of transporting bus loads of people, flood them with traumatic memories and bring them right back and hit them with the second whammy of enforced migration.

"A bunch of things can go wrong after they spend time at NOLA.
Most of them would potentially suffer emotional trauma. They might procure weapons and drugs while prowling the streets. The return trip with this busload could be combustible." Jill had made her case.

The police and the national guards ran a tight ship in the shelters.

She wanted similar services but the contractor did not want to spend money for safety.

She had stood up to them and the plan was benched.

Power brokers danced behind the scenes and came up with a compromise.
Armed protection will be provided and Jill caved in though her gut had misgivings about safety.

The group talked it over and they all wanted to endure this risk and make the journey.

To their surprise, the promised guard did not materialize and in their conspicuous absence they dispatched some brown shirts, the dreaded independent contractors. In the old world they would call mercenaries with no real affiliations or loyalty.

This turn of events infuriated Jill. Many stories of their unprofessional behavior permeated the media chatter and she was reluctant to trust her and others lives with this bunch.

If NOLA PD officers had shot and killed unarmed men on the Danziger Bridge, they would be altar boys compared to this bunch in Brown. Rumors of indiscriminate killing surrounded this outfit.

They did not look very professional. Jill has history of interaction with the military and knew about their integrity which she failed to appreciate in this crowd.

An uneventful path took them in to NOLA. They reached the city by 10 am.
The buses let them off at the canal street

The Canal Street appeared untouched except for a few yellow tarps blowing in the wind from the high rise hotels.

The traffic flowed through Canal Street and so did money into the reconstruction bucket (racket).

The residents were asked to come back to the buses by 6pm near the Sheraton hotel on the Canal Street.

They had 8 hrs to experience NOLA. Jill and Brian had visited the town before but they had had polar opposite experiences.

On the other hand a magical time awaited the seasoned Paul and the wide eyed women.

During her last parlance, the streets had been crowded like the New York. At least this section reassembled a glamorous water hole even with a lot of reconstruction work going on. It looked no different from any American metropolis thoroughfare.

They crossed over to Bourbon Street.
They did not spot any damages.

The shops stayed closed and the tourists had not reached the shores of the Mississippi.

The French quarters had a few musicians playing to sparse crowds.

"Brian do you miss those titty bars?" She pointed out the strip clubs along their way. "You came here for the southern decadence!" A changed Brian laughed at Jill's jab.

They wandered through the" Vieux Carre”
Jill, an expert among others, gave them a bit of history. "The French Quarter is a 78 square-block area, 13 long and 6 deep, bordered by Esplanade Avenue, Canal Street, North Rampart and the Mississippi River."

Jill missed the fine senses she is used to while browsing the Vieux Carre.

"I miss the aroma from a hundred restaurants’ kitchens mingled with the scent of Jasmine and sweet Olives flowers that delicately infused the air and created an intoxicating perfume."

"What are you talking about? Where I came here the last time, I exclusively smelled an obnoxiously pungent odor of human sweat, puke and pee. So much for the inviting romantic southern charm..." Brian countered.

"Was that your scent or that of the street? Did you forget the stench of sex in the dark alleyways?"
Jill appeared to be in a better mood.

They met JC at the intersection of Royal and Dummane Streets.

He played his Sax.

He recognized Jill instantly "Oh my, the sweet duchess." He used to call her Beatrice, the duchess of Milan, while being manic and a Leonardo impersonator.

"This is JC; from the Center at Lafayette."Jill introduced John Connor to others.

"Doc, I am taking all my meds." He bellowed.

"You don't need to announce your private life to the whole French quarters." Jill chided him.
"Let me play a song for the pretty Duchess." he was not short on flirting.
He played a romantic tune for them.

They tipped him and said their goodbyes.

"I hope to run into you again one day Dr. Perkins. You saved my life." His voice spluttered.
"We can dine at the Courtyard of the two sisters when they reopen next year."

"Maybe JC; maybe. It's so far away." Yes it was an eternity away.

Courtyard of two sisters remained closed since the storm but in the French Market, Café de monde opened for business and had been busy.

They ate beignets and drink chicory coffee.

The gruesome pictures, of days immediately following Katrina, became a distant memory for them sitting in the bright sunshine.

In the hustle and bustle of the glamorous NOLA, the nightmares of Katrina got buried.
"This place is not too bad." Brian made a decent note of things.

They walked along the banks of the Mississippi river. It flowed gently as before, without any trace evidence of Katrina's visit.

They went by the ships. The cruise ships now housed clinics, the first responders and relief workers and such. The outer shell of these floating cities only reinforced the glamour though the belly housed agonized souls.

They met a group from SAMHSA.
"You guys have not seen anything here have you?"
"Let us show you around."
The five of them packed into the Minivan and off they went to see the dark side of NOLA.

The other side of the city or the other NOLA or the wrong side of the proverbial tracks (Inter State 10) stayed diagonally opposite to the French quarters and the business district.

Destruction spanned the landscape. Tons of trash and debris piled upon accessible streets. Many areas remained blocked away.

Blocks after block of desertion greeted them.

Downed dead trees created a dead rusty jungle with their brown diseased carcasses. Houses, damaged and gutted had reminder water lines up to the roof.

Hundreds of abandoned cars under the overpasses appeared like a massive pileup in an action thriller. The only missing piece was the river of blood.

The streets mimicked dry river beds, some knee deep in mud and caked up earth. Though no dead bodies floated around at this time, the emptiness of the place sang songs of the death. They visualized the dead abandoned on the curb with piles of the discarded.

They just sat there with dropped jaws, surrounded by total annihilation.

They noted that the Lower ninth ward was the worst hit by the flooding. The breeches in the canal levees had the whole parish under water. Even the highest point in the area was submerged.

Brian talked how the media painted a nasty picture of this community even before the hurricane hit, He reminded the others of the self righteous, who couldn't bring themselves to find an iota of humanity in their hearts and quoted many reasons why the suffering fellow countrymen were at fault and had clamored not to rebuild this ward.

They also had heard about The Wall Street Journal quote that a former Congressman from LA reportedly had told lobbyists, "We finally cleaned up public housing in New Orleans. We couldn't do it, but God did",

Tammy and Brian remembered Tanya as they drove alone New Orleans.

They were speechless on their return.

Jill's had lost her new found cheerfulness.

Sweating and queasy in her stomach, she thought she had seen Mike and Bill in this ruins that resembled bombed out Middle East.

Were they just flash backs or frank visual hallucinations?

They still had some time to kill before the residents returned.

Tammy and Brian went for a walk.

"I like the new Brian." Paul stared at the couple walking away from them.

"He was such a Narcissistic prick when we started out."

A lot of serious stuff happened to him and he appears to be a better person, even he said so."Joanne was impressed.

"I think Tammy is not returning to Florida." Joanne mused.

"Is she going to stay with the Cajun she met.?" Paul asked the other two.

They were confident she would find her way. She had grown during these two weeks.

They sat sipping more French chicory coffee.

"Jill, Joanne and I, had been talking about you"
Jill looked up from reading the tea leaves at the bottom of her coffee cup.

"Oh?"

"Yes" Joanne joined in.

Paul and Joanne in private, made a pitch for their concern.

"Jill, we are worried about you. You know what I mean"

"What are you saying?"

"Both of us witnessed the panic attacks, flash backs and nightmares. We urge you to seek professional help"

"So now you think I am crazy?"

"No we think you have PTSD, We are not sure what your trauma is, but it had a strong effect on your psyche. You are having a significant sequel and this work and the tribulations of the last two weeks are getting to you."

"You are depressed and drink like a fish."

"You initially came across as a level headed person but in the last week, as the nightmares and the flash backs increased, you have become exceedingly irritable and frankly Jill, unstable."

Paul made a synopsis of their thoughts.

"Is that it? Paul, now that I am no longer sweet to you and snapped at you a couple of times, you think I am sick? I am not your wife Paul!"

"Turning to Joanne she said "And as for you missy, just because I let you fuck me, it does not make me crazy."

Paul and Joanne blushed at these retorts from Jill.

She turned to walk away but then stopped and addressed both of them "Joanne you should fuck Paul. He is horny."

Paul, who had no inkling about the nocturnal incident, was not even sure what Jill was talking about.

They were rendered speechless as she continued to walk towards the bus.

The residents tickled back one by one, straggling in like reluctant cattle.

The brown shirts milled around as virtual cowhands, restless and inpatient yet immaturely cocky and with a swagger.

The evening gathered dust and passed into the night.

They stood in groups of 30, one group to each bus.
The brown shirts initiated routine weapons checks.
"Smart thing to do." Jill acknowledged watching from the shadows.

They finished the second bus and moved on to the third when trouble waltzed in. One of the brown shirts found some drugs on one of the residents. Though illegal, they should have been more concerned about weapons and safety. Normally this would go on without much ado.

Unfortunately the chemistry between the two, the greenhorn brown shirt and this middle aged man got toxic right from the beginning.

He came from a forgotten generation that did not considerer pot a drug. To him the young kid was just a punk.

Though, the brown shirt was following the letter of the law, more seasoned soldiers would have handled the situation differently. Jill had watched in appreciation and admiration how those young soldiers and troopers had dealt with situations like this.

This might be the glaring difference between a patriot and a mercenary.

To this brown shirt, this old man was just another junkie looking for trouble.

They came from two different worlds though they shared the same skin color.

Again the fire would have been put out if Jill had remained on top of her game.
But she was on the precipice of her life's chasm.

Unfortunately the tenacious interaction, just before, had made Paul and Joanne a bit on the defensive and distracted.

Brain and Tammy had not returned from their walk.

The pantomime developed in slow motion.

The brown shirt and the middle aged man continued to argue and now were fighting or so she perceived, from where she stood in the shadow of the bus.

There were no human faces expect eerie shadows that danced in the glare of the neon signs that lit up the canal street.

She heard their words over the blare of the car horns.

She saw the gun come out of the holster. He waved the weapon across the man's face….

Her current life and its torture flashed in front of her.
It was a wonderful, cheer filled, youthful life that had been turned upside down by the untimely death.

It all started with the tragic death of her fiancé Captain Mike Tomlinson, MD, US Army, Medical corps.

He was killed in the Mesopotamian desert on the bank of Euphrates.
He laid down his life, the ultimate sacrifice, trying to save lives, when he was blown to smithereens during one of the IED attacks. Even though she was not a witness to the tragedy, her mind had created a virtualization so vivid that it was engraved in her memory for ever as if it had

happened in her presence. The kaleidoscope had changed colors over time except it grew more gruesome and macabre. She became the lone suffering sentinel on the sandy dunes of memory without support from the outside world. In the unrelenting cold vastness of their small bedroom she lay awake every night, thrashing and fighting the unknown demons. She would wake up from the nightmare, and spend the day time alone in the crowd of her peers. Night after night they came back to haunt her.

The sequence of daunting terror remained the same every night. They would be on the London tube. As the train slowed and then stopped at Kings Cross station, the doors flung open and a dozen demonic middle easterners in their long white robes and checkered turbans jumped Mike firing in unison into his head, a thousand shots, bursting his head into a million pieces. Jill's outstretched hands touched splatter of blood. Night after night this sequence continued to molest her mind.

Her dissociation and flashbacks started even before coming to LA. Just the talk of going down to a disaster site transferred her to a world where she had sensed warm blood splattered on her face with Mike drowning in the brackish waters of the lower Ninth.

Her first visit to the Cajun dome sent her into a massive panic attack. It could have been the TV images or the interaction with the National Guard that set it off. But it had started with slight uneasiness that reached the crescendo of a full blown panic attack.

Streams of sweat flowed down the side of her face along her sharp cheek, the ankle of the jaw and on to her blouse. Her heart pounded. Her hands shook and she found it hard to breath, she was light headed and dizzy. She gasped for air and she thought she was having a heart attack, feeling excruciating pain over the sternum. She had been sure she was dying; she had run out to escape. The walls of the building closed around her and she had lost touch with reality.

The tragic deaths of Bill and Tim took its toll.

Bill had been showing evidence of stress and "PTSD" since he returned from Iraq. Bill ended up killing his wife and child and then died by suicide at the hands of the police, something he wished for to happen. Bill was on guard duty at the base one day. In the fading light of a desert day he had shot up a car that did not stop, killing the family of the base electrician, someone he knew. In his mind he had become a monster.
And Tim was barbarously killed in the name of religion and other sins.

She had another panic attack and flash back. The images of Mike and Bill merged into one. The speeding subway collided with the speeding car; the echoes of the tube shattered by the cacophony of M16 rapid fire. Mike lay dead outside the Mercedes shot up by Bill's gun. She had seen Bill shouting at her to stop the car but she was powerless to stop and like a runaway locomotive, she barreled towards Bill and then she was dead, shot up to pieces.

Jill sensed she was losing control of her life. She drank a lot. She had regular flash backs of death. Her nightmares got more complex with juxtaposition of numerous events. She became depressed with all the classic symptoms. Jill began to lose her identity.
Her sexuality transgressed to areas where she had never gone before. She could no longer separate herself from the lives of her patients. She was going in and out of their stories. She was having difficulty differentiating between their past stories and her current reality.

She had finally lost touch with reality.

She had become truly psychotic.

Jill started to move towards the two.

She, Joan de Arc, had to save the world.
"Bill, don't shoot him, can't you see his insignia? He is my husband, Captain Mike Tomlinson." She shouted at the brown shirt. She could not see his face because he had a dancing aquamarine plume on his cap.

They both turned towards her in surprise.

Jill continued her mad rush towards the threat. She did not know if he had a M16 or a Glock. It looked ominous and huge. Frankly, she did not care if he had a sidewinder.

Her Mike was going to be shot up again. "I will not let it happen again, again and again." She wailed like a banshee.

"She desired to stop Bill from killing his wife and child."
"I won't let the police shoot Bill or the prisoner."

"Or Tim sodomized, even though she enjoyed a gory killing of the Cajun women and children in her nightmare."

"I have to save Bill." screamed Jill.
"And Mike, the Cajuns, Tim, and JC and Brian." she continued......

Paul and Joanne were frozen in disbelief.
Brian and Tammy, just walking in, were not even privy to what was happening.

Everything played out in excruciating yet blurry slow motion.

Jill grabbed the gun and everyone except Jill heard the brown shirt say clearly:

"Please let go ma'am."

She only heard the sounds of the thundering subway and the Mercedes and JC's laughter.

The cries of the drowning prisoners and rats rang in her ears.

She continued to wrestle with the brown shirt and his voice was growing urgent and desperate.

"Please ma'am... stop"

A shot ran out..........

The universe came to a grinding halt, followed by echoless silence, as the blood covered young man slowly lowered Jill's lifeless body to the ground.

CHAPTER 23

DAY FOURTEEN

It was their last day, yes, the last day of this tour of duty.

They woke up as usual, but in two minutes, the realization of last night's tragedy hit them like a ton of bricks. They sat on the edge of their beds in total disbelief; it was like waking up from a painful nightmare in reverse.

The group waded in to the dining room like zombies. The new group had taken over the work completely for obvious reasons.

The queen is dead, long live the queen!

For the living, life had to go on…

Paul regained a purpose in his life. He had won a new lease on life and marriage.
He promised to be a clinician through and through.
There was a spring to his step and a fire in his heart.
He was going to catch a plane to Maplewood, MN this evening.
His wife will be waiting to pick him up and drive him home.

Joanne too will go back, back to Eugene Oregon and take a safe cab ride home, to kids and her profession.
She had gained inner strength through her experience and tragedy.
She had a reason to live. She wanted to carry on Jill's legacy.

Tammy decided to stay back.
Jim had already hired her into their fold with welcoming arms.
She will become Cajun with Denis.

Brian sat up at the lunch table, like always, he was the first person to show up.

He shook everyone's hands, hugged Joanne, Tammy Mary and Andrea and left for Tuscan.

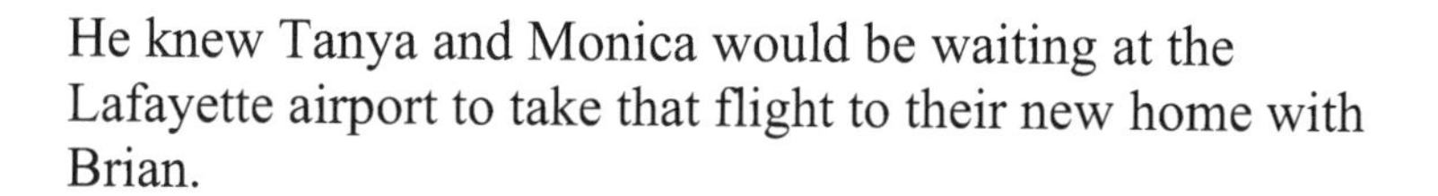
He knew Tanya and Monica would be waiting at the Lafayette airport to take that flight to their new home with Brian.

Andrea and Jim Le Blanc had a hard time,
They adored the whole team especially Jill.
They would have to live through this tragedy.

The same was true for Mary and John.
The death cast gloom over Pellerin residence.

Two couples had lost a daughter!

The authorities promised to finish the autopsy and fly Jill's body to PA.

Yes, for the living, life goes on…..

EPILOGUE

PITTSBURGH, PENNSYLVANIA

Summer of 2006

It was the end of June and the summer was in its full glory. True to the form of the last decade, Pittsburgh had a short wet spring that quickly rolled over to a sunny bright dry summer.

The flowers were still in bloom blissfully unaware of the agony that the last few seasons had come to bear on Oakland.

The double tragedy surrounding the loss of Drs Higgin and Perkins threw the big house and its training program in chaos.

But by the middle of the year the world and the big house had moved on.

It was residents' graduation day.

Walter usually wins the teaching award in his division. Jill had started winning in his footsteps…

Mary used to Joke....

"When are you leaving us Walter? Maybe after you leave, one of us can win that award."

The incoming chief residents were giving away the teaching awards…

The teachers of the year are……..

Dr. Cynthia McAlister, the chief resident, was lost in thought over the spectrum of events that had happened since the last graduation.

She should be overjoyed and exuberant on this occasion. She was finally an attending psychiatrist following the footsteps of her two esteemed mentors, teachers and friends.

But instead she was laden with deep sorrow.

She glanced at the people around her.

Drs. Adele, Rob and Rick, Mary and Eric were all there.

She also noted with a sigh, the two empty seats that seemed larger than life.

Some time ago, she had delivered the eulogy at a special memorial service. She, an accomplished singer, had encapsulated it in a beautiful song, "Bitter end" by Dixie Chicks.

Amidst the cacophony of the voices of the milling crowd, Cynthia heard the same melody.

She saw those two faces in the crowd smiling and beckoning her.

Was she dissociating?

Had the cycle begin all over again?

PICTURES

Unlike the story, these pictures are real!

THE UNIFORM

CHURCH ON ROUTE 27

THE ROAD TO NO WHERE,
HOLLY BEACH

CAJUN DOME
&
CONCENTION CENTER,

LAFAYETTE, LA

STAIRS TO….

DOWN TOWN CAMERON

LETS' BUILD AGAIN….
CAMERON, LA

THE FLEET …

INTERCOASTAL CITY, LA

R.I.P. ....

VERMILLION BAY, LA

EXPRESSIONS

ON BOURBON STREET, NOLA

THE OTHER NOLA

GLAMOROUS CANAL STREET, NOLA

SIGNS OF TIMES…
BOURBON STREET NOLA

MARCH TO JACKSON SQUARE,
NOLA

ANOTHER TRASH DAY…. NOLA

SIGNS OF HUMANITY…. NOLA

DESOLATION THY NAME IS NOLA

WHAT PRICE DO WE PAY FOR GAS?

REMAINS OF A DOCTOR'S OFFICE

HIGHWAY TO?

THE WONDERFUL TEAM 2005

Cajun Glossary

Andouille (ahn-ho-ee_) smoked sausage

Bayou (bai u, bayou): Small slow moving stream or creek in low lying areas. Seen in Mississippi river delta, Home of craw fish, shrimp and cat fish, Lafourche and Bayou des Ecores

Beb sweetheart

Boudin (boo-Dan) pork, rice, onions and garlic sausage fresh

Beignet (ben-yea) fried doughnuts with powdered sugar on top eaten with

Café au lait (café-au-lai) chicory coffee and milk

Chaudin pigs stomach stuffed with spiced pork and smoked

Couche- couche (koosh-koosh) fried corn meal topped with milk and cane syrup

Court bouillon (coo-boo-yon) tomato stew with fish fillet onions and vegetables

Craw fish Very small lobster like shell fish found in the bayou, called mud bugs

Dirty Rice Pan-fried leftover cooked rice sautéed with green peppers, onion, celery, stock, liver, giblets and many other ingredients
Etouffee (ay-too-fay) stew with craw fish or shrimp

File (Fe-lay) Ground sassafras leaves used to season, among other things, gumbo.

Fricassee (free kay say) stew

Gratons pork rinds

Gumbo (gum boe) a thick, roux-based soup sometimes thickened with okra or file'.

Joie de vivre (attitude towards life)

Jambalaya A rice dish with any combination of beef, pork, fowl, smoked sausage, ham, or seafood, as well as celery, green peppers and tomatoes

"Laissez les bon temps rouler" let the good times roll
Praline (prew leen) candy
Po boy sandwich stuffed with fried oysters, shrimp, fish, crawfish, meatballs, smoked sausage and more.

Pod nah good friend
Tasso pork jerky

Turducken deboned turkey stuffed with duck that is stuffed with chicken

Vieux caree (voo-ca-ray) old quarters French quarters

"Make the connection",

United States Veterans Affairs.

Make the Connection *is a public awareness campaign by the U.S. Department of Veterans Affairs (VA) that provides personal testimonials and resources to help Veterans discover ways to improve their lives. Many of our Nation's Veterans—from those who served in World War II to those involved in current conflicts—return not only with physical wounds but also mental health issues they may not recognize.*

REFERENCES

1. 11 Facts about Hurricane Katrina
   Dosomething.org website
2. Eye on the Storm: Hurricane Katrina- Fast Facts.
   Brian Handwerk for National Geographic News.
3. Hurricane Katrina and Rita
   National Oceanic and Atmospheric
   Administration,
   National Climatic Data Center.

- Hurricane Katrina - A Climatological Perspective (NCDC Tech. Report #2005-01)
- NCDC's Tropical Cyclone Overview Page
- Space Science and Engineering Center Hurricane Katrina Page
- The National Weather Service
- NOAA's National Hurricane Center NOAA's Climate Prediction Center.
- *Climate Services and Monitoring Division*
  NOAA/National Climatic Data center
  151 Patton Avenue
  Asheville, NC 28801-5001
  fax: +1-828-271-4876
  phone: +1-828-271-4800
  email: ncdc.info@noaa.gov
  To request climate data, please E-mail:ncdc.orders@noaa.gov

Flood of 1927

- Historian Stephen Ambrose: the Expedition Journal in the "The National Geographic.
- John Barry : Rising Tide: The Great Mississippi Flood of 1927
- and How It Changed America"

I have included below information on PTSD and MST from the **"Make the connection", United States Veterans Affairs, entirely, as a public service, to heighten the nation's awareness of these two problems.**

Post Traumatic Stress disorder (PTSD)

Courtesy:

"Make the connection", United States Veterans Affairs.

What is PTSD?

You feel on edge. Nightmares keep coming back. Sudden noises make you jump. You're staying at home more and more. Could you have PTSD?

If you have experienced severe trauma or a life-threatening event, you may develop symptoms of posttraumatic stress, commonly known as posttraumatic stress disorder, PTSD, shell shock, or combat stress. Maybe you felt like your life or the lives of others were in danger, or that you had no control over what was happening. You may have witnessed people being injured or dying, or you may have been physically harmed yourself.

"Even though I knew they were just fireworks on the 4th of July, to me they still sounded like incoming mortars. It took me right back to my deployment..."

Some of the most common symptoms of PTSD include recurring memories or nightmares of the event(s),sleeplessness, loss of interest, or feeling numb, anger, and irritability, but there are many ways PTSD can impact your everyday life.

Sometimes these symptoms don't surface for months or years after the event or returning from deployment. They may also come and go. If these problems won't go away or are getting worse—or you feel like they are disrupting your daily life—you may have PTSD.

Some factors can increase the likelihood of a traumatic event leading to PTSD, such as:

- The intensity of the trauma
- Being hurt or losing a loved one
- Being physically close to the traumatic event
- Feeling you were not in control
- Having a lack of support after the event

What are the signs of PTSD?

"Driving down the roads in my home town, I found myself noticing every piece of debris, avoiding every pothole."

A wide variety of symptoms may be signs you are experiencing PTSD:

- Feeling upset by things that remind you of what happened
- Having nightmares, vivid memories, or flashbacks of the event that make you feel like it's happening all over again
- Feeling emotionally cut off from others
- Feeling numb or losing interest in things you used to care about
- Becoming depressed
- Thinking that you are always in danger
- Feeling anxious, jittery, or irritated
- Experiencing a sense of panic that something bad is about to happen

- Having difficulty sleeping
- Having trouble keeping your mind on one thing
- Having a hard time relating to and getting along with your spouse, family, or friends

"When stress brought on flashbacks, I dealt with them by drinking them away. I considered it recreational drinking, but really I was self-medicating."

It's not just the symptoms of PTSD but also how you may react to them that can disrupt your life. You may:

- Frequently avoid places or things that remind you of what happened
- Consistent drinking or use of drugs to numb your feelings
- Consider harming yourself or others
- Start working all the time to occupy your mind
- Pull away from other people and become isolated

What is the treatment for PTSD?

If you have PTSD, it doesn't mean you just have to live with it. In recent years, researchers from around the world have dramatically increased our understanding of what causes PTSD and how to treat it. Hundreds of thousands of Veterans have gotten treatment for PTSD—and treatment works.

"In therapy I learned how to respond differently to the thoughts that used to get stuck in my head."

Two types of treatment have been shown to be effective for treating PTSD: counseling and medication. Professional counseling can help you understand your thoughts and discover ways to cope with your feelings. Medications, called selective serotonin reuptake inhibitors, are used to help you feel less worried or sad.

In just a few months, these treatments can produce positive and meaningful changes in symptoms and quality of life. They can help you understand and change how you think about your trauma—and change how you react to stressful memories.

You may need to work with your doctor or counselor and try different types of treatment before finding the one that's best for dealing with your PTSD symptoms.

What can I do if I think I have PTSD?

"I wanted to keep the war away from my family, but I brought the war with me every time I opened the door. It helps to talk with them about how I feel."

In addition to getting treatment, you can adjust your lifestyle to help relieve PTSD symptoms. For example, talking with other Veterans who have experienced trauma can help you connect with and trust others, exercising can help reduce physical tension and volunteering can help you reconnect with your community. You also can let your friends and family know when certain places or activities make you uncomfortable.

Your close friends and family may be the first to notice that you're having a tough time. Turn to them when you are ready to talk. It can be helpful to share what you're experiencing, and they may be able to provide support and help you find treatment that is right for you.

Take the next step – Make the connection.

Whether you just returned from a deployment or have been home for 40 years, it's never too late to get professional treatment or support for PTSD. Receiving counseling or treatment as soon as possible can keep your symptoms from getting worse. Even Veterans who did not realize they had PTSD for many years have benefited from treatment that allows them to deal with their symptoms in new ways.

You can also consider connecting with:

- Your family doctor: Ask if your doctor has experience treating Veterans or can refer you to someone who does
- A mental health professional, such as a therapist
- Your local VA Medical Center or Vet Center: VA specializes in the care and treatment of Veterans
- A spiritual or religious advisor

"I thought I was being brave by ignoring it. But I was really being brave by facing up to it."

In addition, taking a self-assessment can help you find out if your feelings and behaviors may be related to PTSD. This short list of questions won't be able to tell you for sure whether or not you have PTSD, but it may indicate whether it's a good idea to see a professional for further assessment. If you believe you may be living with PTSD and are ready to take the next step, find a professional near you who may be able to help.

Explore these resources for more information about PTSD in Veterans

Vet Centers

If you are a combat Veteran or experienced any sexual trauma during your military service, bring your DD214 to

your local Vet Center and speak with a counselor or therapist—many of whom are Veterans themselves—for free, without an appointment, and regardless of your enrollment status with VA.
http://www2.va.gov/directory/guide/vetcenter_flsh.asp

Understanding PTSD Booklet
This eight-page booklet explains what PTSD is, provides information and resources on support, and shares real stories from people who have dealt effectively with PTSD.
http://www.ptsd.va.gov/public/understanding_ptsd/booklet.pdf

Understanding PTSD Treatment
This eight-page booklet explains in detail the various proven ways to treat PTSD and debunks some myths about treatment.
http://www.ptsd.va.gov/public/understanding_TX/booklet.pdf

National Center for PTSD
Explore this comprehensive website for detailed information about PTSD, its effects and treatment, and resources for support.
www.ptsd.va.gov/public/index.asp

VA's PTSD Program Locator
This site will allow you to search for PTSD programs located near you. If you are eligible to receive care through the Veterans Health Administration, you can enroll in one of VA's PTSD treatment programs.
http://www2.va.gov/directory/guide/ptsd_flsh.asp

Military Sexual Trauma

(MST)

Courtesy

"Make the connection", United States Veterans Affairs

"During their service, both female and male Service members sometimes have upsetting, unwanted sexual experiences, including sexual assault or sexual harassment. "Military sexual trauma" or MST is the term used by the U.S. Department of Veterans Affairs to refer to these experiences. The official definition of MST used by VA is given by federal law (U.S. Code 1720D of Title 38). It is:

Psychological trauma, which in the judgment of a VA mental health professional, resulted from a physical assault of a sexual nature, battery of a sexual nature, or sexual harassment which occurred while the Veteran was serving on active duty or active duty for training.

Sexual harassment is defined as "repeated, unsolicited verbal or physical contact of a sexual nature which is threatening in character."

In more concrete terms, MST includes any sexual activity where you were involved against your will. You may have been physically forced into sexual activities. Or, no physical force may have been used but you were coerced or pressured into sexual activities. For example, you may have been threatened with negative consequences for refusing to cooperate. Or it may have been suggested that you would get faster promotions or better treatment in exchange for sex. MST also includes sexual experiences that happened while you were not able to consent to sexual activities, such as if you were intoxicated. Other MST experiences include unwanted sexual touching or grabbing, threatening, offensive remarks about your body or your sexual activities, and threatening and unwelcome sexual advances. If these experiences occurred while you were on active duty or active duty for training, they are considered to be MST.

"I remember the faces, the words, the smells, the negative, and the unwarranted, unsolicited touches. I remember all of that. And I have friends who also are Veterans and went through worse than I did."

It's important to know that MST can occur on or off base, and while a Service member is on or off duty. Perpetrators can be men or women, military personnel or civilians, superiors or subordinates in the chain of command. They may have been a stranger to you, or even a friend or intimate partner. Veterans from all eras of service have reported experiencing MST.

If you experienced military sexual assault or harassment, you may blame yourself or feel ashamed. It is important to remember that MST is not your fault. Nothing ever justifies someone harassing or assaulting you.

How can MST affect Veterans?

MST is an experience, not a diagnosis or a condition in and of itself. Because of this, Veterans may react in a wide variety of ways to experiencing MST. Problems may not surface until months or years after the MST, and sometimes not until after a Veteran has left military service. For some Veterans, experiences of MST may continue to affect their mental and physical health, work, relationships, and everyday life even many years later.

Your reaction may depend on factors such as:

- Whether you have a prior history of trauma
- The types of responses you received from others at the time of the experience
- Whether the experience happened once or was repeated over time

Some of the difficulties both female and male survivors of MST may have include:

Strong emotions: feeling depressed; having intense, sudden emotional responses to things; feeling angry or irritable all the time

Feelings of numbness: feeling emotionally 'flat'; trouble feeling love or happiness

Trouble sleeping: trouble falling or staying asleep; bad dreams or nightmares

Trouble with attention, concentration, and memory: trouble staying focused; often finding your mind wandering; having a hard time remembering things

Problems with alcohol or other drugs: drinking to excess or using drugs daily; getting drunk or "high" to cope with memories or unpleasant feelings; drinking to fall asleep

Trouble with reminders of the sexual trauma: feeling on edge or 'jumpy' all the time; not feeling safe; going out of your way to avoid reminders of the trauma; trouble trusting others

Problems in relationships: feeling alone or not connected to others; abusive relationships; trouble with employers or authority figures

Physical health problems: sexual issues; chronic pain weight or eating problems; stomach or bowel problems

Fortunately, people can recover from experiences of trauma, and VA has services to help Veterans move their lives forward.

Why can MST be so harmful?

Sexual assault is more likely to result in symptoms of posttraumatic stress disorder (PTSD) than are most other types of trauma, including combat. Also, the experience of MST can differ from the experience of other traumas, and even from the experience of sexual trauma in the civilian world. Why is this?

"Going through a sexual assault is bad enough. Then to have this happen to me in my job as a soldier; it was really difficult because what happened to the unit support? Your fellow soldiers are supposed to have your back."

Factors that may be unique to MST include:

- You may have had to continue to live and work with your perpetrator, and even rely on him or her for essential things like food, health care, or watching your back on patrol
- You may have been worried about damaging the team spirit of your unit if your perpetrator was in the same unit

- You may have been worried about appearing weak or vulnerable, and thoughts that others would not respect you
- You may have thought that if others found out, it would end your career or your chances for promotion

For these and other reasons, the experience of MST can put Service members in some no-win situations and be emotionally difficult for them to resolve as Veterans.

What should I know about treatment and VA services?

Although MST can be a very difficult experience, there are treatments available that can significantly improve your quality of life. Treatment often involves addressing any immediate health and safety concerns, followed by counseling to help you learn new ways of thinking, practice positive behaviors, and take active steps to cope with the effects of MST. Treatment may focus on strategies for coping with difficult emotions and memories or, for Veterans who are ready, treatment may involve actually talking about the MST experiences in depth.

At VA, Veterans can receive free, confidential treatment for mental and physical health conditions related to MST. You may be able to receive this MST-related care even if you are not eligible for other VA services. To receive these services, you do not need a VA service-connected disability rating, and you don't need to have reported the incident when it happened nor to have other documentation that it occurred.

Knowing that MST survivors may have special concerns, every VA healthcare facility has an MST Coordinator who can answer any questions you might have about VA's MST services. VA has a range of services available to meet Veterans where they are in their recovery process:

- Every VA healthcare facility has providers knowledgeable about treatment for problems related MST. Many have specialized outpatient mental health services focusing on sexual trauma. Vet Centers also have specially trained sexual trauma counselors.
- VA has over twenty programs nationwide that offer specialized MST treatment in a residential or inpatient setting. These programs are for Veterans who need more intense treatment and support.
- Because some Veterans do not feel comfortable in mixed-gender treatment settings, some facilities have separate programs for men and women. All residential and inpatient MST programs have separate sleeping areas for men and women.

What can I do to help manage my reactions to my experiences of MST?

"You can find the plan and techniques that work for you. What worked for me may not work for you but I can tell you I found the steps that led to my recovery: going to VA, asking about their options, talking to somebody about my MST and PTSD, going to their classes, attending their groups."

If you're having problems related to your experiences of MST, you should consider seeking support from a doctor or counselor. In addition, there are many things you can do on your own to heal and recover after MST. Some basic lifestyle changes can have a positive impact on your overall well-being. Try to:

- Get a good night's sleep
- Maintain a healthy diet by eating right
- Seek medical advice for any health concerns
- Avoid excessive use of alcohol
- Take over-the-counter and prescription drugs only as directed by your doctor
- Avoid illegal drug use
- Avoid risky behavior, like unsafe sex, gambling, and reckless driving
- Recognize triggers—keep a record to help identify situations that are more likely to worsen your symptoms
- Take up a new hobby or a recreational activity that can be a healthy way to fill your time
- Talk to others—this can help you from feeling isolated and give friends and loved ones a chance to help you
- Exercise regularly
- Practice relaxation techniques such as breathing exercises, meditation, or prayer

Your close family and friends may notice that you're having a tough time. If you feel comfortable, you may want to talk to them about what you're experiencing. They may be able to provide support and help you find treatment that is right for you.

You can also take a confidential and anonymous self-assessment about your reactions. This short list of questions may help you decide how important it is to see a professional for further evaluation.

Take the next step — Make the connection.

Every day, Veterans connect with helpful resources and effective treatments for MST-related issues that help them improve their lives. It can be difficult to deal with the problems caused by MST on your own, so talking to your family and friends can be an important first step. You can also consider connecting with:

- Your family doctor: Ask if your doctor has experience treating Veterans with sexual trauma or can refer you to someone who does
- A mental health professional, such as a therapist or counselor
- Your local VA Medical Center or Vet Center: VA specializes in the care and treatment of Veterans and every VA Medical Center has a Military Sexual Trauma Coordinator on site who can work with you. Vet Centers also have staff who are specially trained to help with the effects of Military Sexual Trauma
- A spiritual or religious advisor
- A Sexual Assault Response Counselor (SARC) – if you are an Active Duty or National Guard Service member, SARCs are available 24/7 every day of the year to help you decide if you want to officially report your trauma and to help you get care. Each branch of the military has Sexual Assault Response Counselors that you can contact through Military OneSource (1-800-342-9647)

Wanting to harm you or having thoughts of suicide are very serious concerns and need immediate attention. It's important you talk to someone right away if you have thoughts of death or suicide. If you are thinking about death or suicide, call the Veterans Crisis Line at 1-800-273-8255 or use the confidential Veterans Crisis Line online chat. Both services provide free, confidential support, 24 hours a day, seven days a week.

Explore these resources for more information about MST and its effects in Veterans.

Learn more about how MST may be related to other issues such as relationship problems, alcohol or drug problems, depression, and posttraumatic stress.

Afterdeployment.org
Take an online sexual trauma assessment to evaluate how you are handling your experiences of MST. You can also hear from other Veterans and Service members dealing with MST, and learn more about how MST may be related to issues such as relationship problems, posttraumatic stress, depression, and excessive use of alcohol/drugs.
http://afterdeployment.org/web/guest/topics-military-sexual-trauma

VA Office of Mental Health Services – MST Support Team
This website provides information on VA's programs and services for treating MST.
http://www.mentalhealth.va.gov/msthome.asp

VA Medical Center Facility Locator
This website will allow you to search for VA programs located near you. You can contact your nearest VA Medical Center to speak with a MST Coordinator and learn about your treatment options. Veterans, members of the National Guard, and Reservists can receive free, confidential treatment at VA for mental and physical health conditions related to MST. You may be able to receive this care even if you are not eligible for other VA services. To receive free MST-related services, you do not need a VA service-connected disability rating, to have reported the incident when it happened, or have other documentation that it

occurred.
http://www2.va.gov/directory/guide/home.asp?isflash=1

Vet Centers
If you are a combat Veteran or experienced any sexual trauma during your military service, bring your DD214 to your local Vet Center and speak with a counselor or therapist—many of whom are Veterans themselves—for free, without an appointment, and regardless of your enrollment status with VA.

http://www2.va.gov/directory/guide/vetcenter_flsh.asp

Veterans Crisis Line
1-800-273-8255 PRESS 1

Since 1974, this flag has officially identified the Acadians who migrated to Louisiana.

Courtesy CBC

Made in the USA
Charleston, SC
09 March 2013